Interactive Press

Memento Mori

Daniel King, who also writes as "David King", was born in Western Australia and has lived there all his life. He holds degrees in Engineering and English, and a Doctorate in Philosophy. Daniel's first literary publication was in 1986, and since then he has had over fifty stories (and also, in recent years, poetry) published in various Australian and overseas journals.

Interactive Press
The Literature Series

Memento Mori

Daniel King

Interactive Press
Brisbane

Interactive Press
an imprint of IP (Interactive Publications Pty Ltd)
Treetop Studio • 9 Kuhler Court
Carindale, Queensland, Australia 4152
sales@ipoz.biz
ipoz.biz/IP/IP.htm

First published by IP in 2010

Printed in 11 pt Book Antiqua on 16 pt Book Antiqua by Griffin Press.

National Library of Australia
Cataloguing-in-Publication data:

Author: King, Daniel.

Title: Memento mori / Daniel King.

ISBN: 9781921479427 (pbk.)

Dewey Number: A823.4

Memento Mori

Acknowledgements

Jacket Image: Sebastian Kaulitzki

Jacket Design: David Reiter

Author Photo: Kristy Mannix Photography

The following stories have either been published before or are due to be published:

"Memento Mori" (*FourW* 19, 2008, pp. 108-114); "Nothing Contemplates Nothing" (*FourW* 17, 2006, pp. 9-14); "Your Pain is My Pain" (*FourW* 20, 2009, pp. 83-89); "Heaven and/or Hell" (*FourW* 18, 2007, pp. 10-15); "A Dream Holiday" (*RE:AL* 25/1, 2000, pp. 155-161); "Tim's Howse" (*Redoubt* 2, 1988, pp. 18-21); "Myths of the K Mart" (*LiNQ* 14/3, 1986, pp. 82-85); "Another Fall Myth" (*Dirigible* 12, 1998, pp. 14-17); "Going Back" (*LiNQ* 15/2, 1987, pp. 54-57); "Open to the Sky" (*FourW* 15, 2004, pp. 105-108); "Dreams Never End" (*Mattoid* 57 forthcoming); "Catenary" (*FourW* 12, 2001, pp. 129-133).

Special thanks are owed to the editors of *FourW* for awarding me their "Best Story" prizes for "Nothing Contemplates Nothing" and "Heaven and/or Hell"; and to Interactive Publications for awarding this collection a High Commendation in IP Picks 2010.

Contents

Memento Mori

1

As Professor Ken Rivers eased himself into the large, antique, stone-pine dresser in the spare room, he felt a growing sense of peace. Over the last few months Connie had put him under such pressure with regard to cosmetic surgery that if he hadn't been able to hide in the dresser occasionally he probably would have had a complete breakdown by now. He ran his fingers over the mild, reassuring wood. He knew that hiding in the dresser represented, in Freudian terms, a return to the womb – but if it helped him to cope, why shouldn't he hide?

He listened. Had the front door opened? Connie was supposed to be at her third year Shakespeare tutorial until four, but often the tutorials finished early. Many students found her manner domineering, and wouldn't stay for the whole three hours. The absenteeism was accentuated towards the end of semester when students took time off to finish their already-overdue essays.

Deciding not to run the risk that she would catch him in the dresser, he climbed out and brushed some motes from his charcoal suit.

The door opened. "Oh, Ken. What a relief." Connie cast a pile of lever arch files and textbooks on to the spare bed and made an exhausted, exasperated sigh. "Honestly, I don't know why students bother to enroll in units if they're not going to attend tutorials. I had a really interesting discussion planned on the subject of whether, given Kant's *Third Critique*, we can still talk about the 'timeless beauty' of Shakespeare's sonnets

1

and only two students deigned to attend! Of course, both of them were exchange students, so I had to do all the talking. I can't think how they expect to pass. They just have no interest in looking to the future."

Ken smiled weakly. "I think you'll find most students are too politically savvy these days to swallow arguments about timeless beauty. You might just as well talk about God."

She peered at him as though over the top of a pair of glasses. Long ago she had worn glasses but radial keratotomy had obviated the need for them. "Is this yet another way of trying to get me to drop the subject of cosmetic surgery? Really, Ken, for a philosopher you're remarkably conventional sometimes." She clicked dismissively, her red eyebrows curving like rearing snakes. "People spend thousands of dollars on holidays, which are over practically as soon as they've begun, yet they agonise about spending a bit of money for something with years of benefits."

"But I don't see why I should have to go under the knife. I want to grow old gracefully."

"You're saying 'gracefully' when you mean 'gradually'. There's nothing graceful about decay."

"Well – and I've asked you this many times, without getting a satisfactory reply – why do you want me to change my appearance? I'm the same person I always was."

"Oh, so the idea of timeless *beauty* is nonsense, but the idea of timeless *personhood* is not!" Connie was triumphant. "Call yourself a philosopher!"

"I'm just saying what they believe." Ken felt hurt – deeply hurt. Connie had many times criticised his physical appearance but never his mind. It was the last bond between them, really (apart from sex – he had a very high libido and found her, when she wasn't being obsessive about cosmetic surgery, overwhelmingly sexually attractive). Numbly, he realised that he was staring at the crotch of her slacks. Normally, this would have aroused him but now its Y-shaped creases reminded him of a skeletal hand. No doubt her mocking mood was responsible. He wondered absently whether she'd had yet another *contretemps* with the Dean.

She gestured to him much as she would to a very young child. "Look at me, Ken. I've had cosmetic surgery many, many times. How old would you say I looked? Thirty-five? Thirty? And yet I'm in my late fifties! Wouldn't you like to share in that experience? You could start off with a minor procedure, like lower-lid blepharoplasty. Surely you don't want to be a memento mori for me!" She went to the dresser and looked in its mirror. Patted her rich, dyed-auburn hair, which framed her attractive, elliptical face. "Yes, I could easily pass for thirty."

"I find the whole idea of dwelling on age almost astrological." Surprised, almost alarmed by his boldness, Ken pressed on, "A year simply marks the amount of time the sun takes to pass through all the constellations of the Zodiac, its apparent radial motion." Again he smiled weakly. "Perhaps some of the more New Age students have been influencing you, my dear."

Connie narrowed her already thin lips, then licked them. She enjoyed a verbal duel. "But that's just the point. Age measured in years is irrelevant. All that counts is quality of appearance and quality of intellect and we must strive to maintain both."

"In that order, no doubt." He made a vague motion with his hand. "We'll talk about this some more later, if we must. I want to do some work on my paper now."

When he was sure that Connie had left the room (and he felt that he would be able to have at least a couple of hours by himself), he gathered together some books, a pen and some sheets of foolscap. Then he eased himself into the dresser once more and prepared to write. Her allusion to Kant had made him wonder whether he could write a kind of philosophical treatise to come to terms with his dilemma concerning cosmetic surgery. The writing would be in his usual style: a style like that of fiction, with him as a character. He'd call it "Memento Mori", after a dry poem he'd written a few years ago about Connie's ideas. He might even use the same pen-name he'd adopted for the poem. The point of writing this way was that the ideas would emerge almost as though in dialogue form. He estimated that he could produce at least eight pages on the subject.

2

Ken jumped. His glasses must have slipped from his nose! Where were they? He glanced absently at the grandmother clock. Five o'clock.

Suddenly realising that he shouldn't be able even to see the clock without his glasses, he gave it his full attention. It had been fitted with an electric movement, which he always felt didn't suit the house's decor; and he could perceive part of the battery wires in sharp relief against the wood. What had happened? He regarded his hands and was astonished to see that all their grey hairs had gone. They were smooth and bore no trace of age-spots.

Feeling a sudden cold panic that the dreaded breakdown might at last be upon him, he climbed out of the dresser. Immediately, he knew that he had indeed undergone a change. His body felt lighter, more spritely. Was this typical of mental breakdowns? He turned apprehensively to face the cheval mirror on the other side of the room and was astounded to see that the familiar stooped body with its too-baggy suit, benign expression, widow's peak and bespectacled watery eyes had been replaced by the wiry frame of a boy in his late teens.

He turned, as though expecting to see the owner of this youthful body standing behind him, his own mature body transparent. But he was the room's only inhabitant. He looked down at his legs, kneaded them. They were skinny and clad in jeans rather than a suit. He moved closer to the mirror, tantalisingly repelled by the rather impish expression that stared back at him. Oddly, he felt as though he were rereading a book that had once been very familiar to him.

And then he knew why. The figure in the mirror was Ken Rivers as a seventeen year-old.

"Connie." His throat was dry. "Could you come please? Something has happened." Fumbling for the steel door knob, he made his way to the kitchen. Connie, he knew, would be flinging saucepan lids and vegetable strainers about, preparing her usual post-tutorial chilli omelette.

"Yes, what is it? I'm flat out here."

He stepped into the kitchen. "Look."

"Oh!" Her face appeared simultaneously startled, entranced and strangely piqued. "Who are you?"

"Ken. Your husband." He felt an annoyed desperation. "Please help me, Connie." He held his head. Had his thoughts too taken on a youthful naivety, a brashness? But didn't such questioning, by virtue of its mature and restrained reflectiveness, answer the question in the negative? On the other hand, his thoughts had been mature even as a seventeen year-old.

Connie made an arch expression. "This is unexpected, but welcome." She went to him and he was struck then by how old she looked. It was as though she had never had cosmetic surgery at all. But after the shock of his own apparent transformation, this amounted to no more than a mild surprise.

She ran a hand up and down his leg. "Which of my courses are you enrolled in?"

"Connie, please don't mess around. I'm glad that you like my new – or is it old? – appearance but I think I'm having a breakdown." He held his head, confounded. "Can you actually hear what I'm saying?"

"It was the unit on Iser last year, wasn't it? Or were you there when I delivered my paper 'Realist Fiction: Conventions and Clichés'? Don't worry, you won't be the first student who's made a pass. I like guys in their late teens. You'd be astonished if you knew how old I am! But we'll have to go somewhere else. My husband is around somewhere."

"You... you've committed adultery?" Suddenly, Ken realised that she wasn't joking.

"My philosophy is that no person is the same two days in a row, so you might as well have the odd fling with people who are obviously different!"

For a few moments Ken merely stared at her. Then he hastened forward, violating her space. "Whore! Why must you continually mock me? Sex and love are inseparable!" He attempted to grasp her hands with his, trying not to become aroused as he did so, but they felt unfamiliar and his emotions were strangely getting in the way. Alarmed, Connie reeled against the stove. She seized a heavy strainer and swung it against his head.

Ken staggered off the floor, the room appearing to tip back and forth as though it were mounted on a see-saw. He steadied himself with a kitchen chair. How long had he been unconscious? His head was still pounding, so presumably Connie's blow had been quite recent.

He sat on the chair. Everything that had happened seemed oddly remote. He was surprised to realise that he found the revelation of Connie's adultery even more shocking than the transformation of his body into that of his seventeen year-old self. It was like a blow to his very existence, he thought, a denial that the person he referred to as "Ken Rivers" had any kind of continuing link with his earlier selves – selves that she had found desirable and to which, presumably, she had once been committed.

He held his hands in front of him and with an infinite relief, which was nevertheless tinged with a stabbing sadness, saw that they were the familiar gnarled appendages again, the fingers like the wrinkled larvae of some large moth.

So had he imagined everything?

"Connie...!" He paused, wondering what to say to her. Would she still be angry with him? But it was he who should be angry with her – assuming of course, that there was any element of reality in the events he remembered. And perhaps there wasn't. Reality, he had often taught, was inter-subjective, the product of people, not just of one person.

There was no reply. Gingerly, he stood, began to wander around the kitchen, opening cupboards as he went. All the cooking utensils were in place. There was no evidence either of Connie's post-tutorial chilli omelette or of her attacking him. He picked up a couple of folded pieces of paper she must have dropped. One was his "Memento Mori" poem:

Memento Mori
by
D.K.

Between the eyes,
Eternal perfect circles,
And the teeth,
Jagged like tombstones in their temporality,
There is pale clay for the cosmetic surgeon's craft.
Cosmetic surgery is cheap;
Cosmetic surgery is chic.
Yet you, my aging love,
Reject it;
And every evening with a numbness not of anaesthesia
I see your jowls sag lower,
Your cheeks retreat,
Drawing your skull towards your skin,
Thus cruelly condemning me to life with a memento mori.
A few defining lines,
A few quick cuts:
And time would be redeemed.
Alas!
The only cuts are to my soul.

He tried to remember if he had been alluding to the well-known "otherness", and thus inevitable decay and aging, said by theorists to characterise the semiotic reader-writer relationship. Giving up, he looked at the other piece of paper. It was Connie's class attendance list, with only two names ticked. He smiled to himself, feeling a sudden warmth – surely it was not just a sad empathy? – for her. He mused that he really did owe her something for putting up with his conservativeness, his imaginings. Apart from her obsession with cosmetic surgery (he smiled to think he had even considered the possibility of her adultery) she was an ideal wife. Experiencing a slight arousal, he adjusted his trousers.

"Connie...!"

He stepped into the laundry and was startled to see, crouched beside the washing-machine, a girl of about nine. She was wearing a red dress and a rather old-fashioned hair ribbon, in the shape of a moth, with strawberry emblems. "Who are you?"

The girl said something but he couldn't quite make out her words.

"I'm sorry. You'll have to say that again." Ken peered at her, trying to seem kindly. There was something familiar about the girl. The highly-curved eyebrows, the elliptical face, the thin lips, a certain lack of grace....

And then he knew. It was Connie as a child. He remembered seeing in an album years ago – was it over at her mother's? – a photograph of a girl with an identical hair ribbon. She was unmistakably the same person.

He crouched down to her level. "You're Connie, aren't you?"

The girl avoided his eyes, muttered something. She clearly didn't want to talk, although this was obviously due to petulance rather than apprehension.

A part of him wondering how he could accept her transformation so calmly (was *this* the breakdown?), he said, "Did you know, Connie, that one day you and I are going to be married? We're what's known as an ideal couple, absolutely suited to each other in a timeless, transcendent way." He knelt back. "But I suppose you're not familiar with the meaning of those words? Although I know you were an intelligent child."

The girl said nothing, folded her arms.

Suddenly overcome by passion and an awareness that at last the subject of cosmetic surgery would not arise, he reached firmly for the child. Began to kiss her. She struggled, but he held her even more tightly.

"Don't mess about, Connie. Love is eternal, a union of persons, stretching from the beginning of time to its end. Even the Church appreciates that." Ken placed his lips firmly on the child's, eased them apart with his tongue. Against it, her reluctant teeth were like tiny smooth river pebbles. He reached for her nonexistent breasts. Then, grasping her wrists behind her back with one hand, he slowly began to undo her dress with the other.

Nothing Contemplates Nothing

1

The house seemed both new and old, Matt thought, as he dragged the last crate into the lounge. It was new in the sense that he had just moved in but it was old in the sense that someone had recently died there, and death always seemed to him to give things an archaic feel.

He glanced around, catching his breath. He would be happier, he realised, if he had been told exactly where the person had died. But the estate agent hadn't known or hadn't been prepared to say. All that he had claimed to know was that somewhere in the house the previous tenant – an amateur writer like himself – had committed suicide, that the body had not been found for nine days and that two fumigations had been required to clear the house of the stench. He concentrated, morbidly fascinated by the idea that a trace of the smell might remain. But it was daylight and the abundance of visual and aural distractions made concentrating on smells difficult. It would probably be different at night, he told himself – and then wished he hadn't.

He glanced around the room again, hating the idea of all the unpacking. Fortunately, rudimentary furnishings – not those belonging to the previous tenant, he had been assured – had been provided, so any exertion would be minimal. In the lounge, which had a low ceiling, the furnishings included blinds of an insipid buff colour; faded armchairs the seams of which were leaking a substance like wood shavings; a futuristic plastic sideboard trimmed with gilt; and a dangling light bulb the shade of which had pale circles suggesting the recent presence of fly-spots.

Suddenly overwhelmingly tired, he sat on the floor. He was not superstitious, but the idea of living in a house where someone had died really did worry him. Every time he looked in the bathroom mirror, he knew, he would be half-expecting to see in front of him a face. Further, every time he took a step within the house he would know that his passage bore an exact, mathematical relationship to the last resting-place, wherever it was, of the previous tenant. As on other occasions, he wondered whether he was mentally disturbed. He quickly told himself that the problem was not with him but with the house. If only he had a job, he wouldn't have to rely on rented accommodation! But he'd never been able to cope with nine-to-five employment. Whenever he had tried it, his mind had wandered: sometimes he had felt as though he could actually move back and forth through time. Forgetting things. And as a result of having no job he was poor. The only consolation was that it was summer, and he would not have to worry about heating bills.

Closing his eyes, he began to pull items from the crate closest to him.

2

Later that night, he sat at his typewriter. He stared at the ceiling, and then at the door. Just as in his flat, his last home (the constant interruption of neighbours had driven him out), he couldn't seem to come up with an idea for a story. Noticing his shaving mirror to the left of the typewriter, he moved it out of his line of sight, then moved it back. The only way he would conquer his apprehension of living in the house, he realised, would be to confront directly his greatest worry: that of suddenly seeing a face in the mirror. He glanced at the mirror. No face was visible, of course.

He still felt uncertain. Soon, it would be time to go to bed and for all he knew the suicide had taken place in the bedroom itself. And even if it hadn't, tiny traces of the putrefying remains must still be present throughout the house, despite the fumigation. The removal of every atom that had belonged to the body was, after all, scientifically impossible. He remembered reading the statistical reasons for this when he had been researching the article he had hoped to sell to *Science Digest*. All at once, he wondered why he persisted with his writing. Unless he were to write a bestseller, any financial gain would be slight and his approach was too whimsical for the really influential journals. Freud, he reflected, believed that writing was a form of wish-fulfillment, but his only conscious wish at present was learning how to cope with living in the house.

Could he write a story that was actually about coming to terms with living in the house? He stared into the distance, suddenly optimistic. He could set down on paper all possibilities, from the far-fetched to the likely; then he would have dealt with the worst that could happen to him.

Trying not to be concerned by the fact that Borges's story "The Secret Miracle" had explored a similar idea, he began to write.

3

It was night. He sat up. A smell like that of decayed fish kept wafting into his nose. He glanced at the window but it was shut. So not only was there no breeze but also the smell was coming from within the house. He tried to tell himself that the kitchen tidy could not have been closed properly but he knew that that was not the explanation.

He turned on the bedlight and the fluorescent tube gave out a feeble light: a pale, moon-like aura that often illuminated his dreams. Clearly, the tube was almost spent. He climbed out of bed, reached for the door-handle.

The smell of fish was stronger in the passage. He turned right and the smell diminished. Reversing his direction, he found that he was approaching the lounge.

As he turned into the lounge, he stopped, surprised. The floor had become a kind of grating... Gingerly, he moved closer.

The floor had not become a grating. It was just that a number of floorboards parallel to one another had been prised up. He felt an apprehensive puzzlement. Had someone hidden illegal items such as drugs under the floorboards, and had only just had the opportunity to retrieve them?

He narrowed his eyes. There was someone standing beside the hole! Fortunately, he seemed to have his back to him. Apprehensively, he edged behind the figure. No, he was wrong. The figure was *in* the hole. But why was it swaying? Was it searching for something?

And then he saw the rope, and the tongue swollen and sticking out as if in mindless impertinence.

4

He contemplated the page in front of him, and realised he was dissatisfied. Could anything written about the macabre be anything but a cliché? But what did 'cliché' really mean? That which was a cliché in literary writing might merely be a convention in horror fiction. He checked the time. He needed some rest. How long had he been working? And was it the first night or the second? As soon as he had thought this, he felt angry with himself. Again, he thought, he lacked concentration, wandering backwards and forwards in his thoughts (if not in time!).

He needed to be realistic. He would write a sensible, realist piece, in which corpses were merely metaphors for his not having succeeded in life. Perhaps he could allude to his nine year relationship with Anne (Anne the indefinite article, he had called her, just before he walked out on her). The moment in their relationship he most often dwelt on was in the middle of their first January, when he had introduced her to astronomy. He had said to himself, I know that you will never leave me and that I shall never lose you. True, she had never left him but some years later – no, almost half a decade later! – he had been shocked one morning to notice how much her appearance and personality had changed and he had realised in despair that he had lost her after all.

So he would be the central character. There would be no ghost. No death. No body.

But there would be dreams.

5

His head was so heavy.... Trying to keep his eyes open, he saw that he was standing in his dressing-gown in the passage leading to the lounge. Was everything he had been thinking about Anne and writing just an illusion, and had he – surely not! – really murdered a child and buried it beneath the floorboards? The idea was in his head, certainly, but the source was obscure, indefinite. He shook his head. He was not sure to whom the child belonged, or why he had done whatever he had done to it, or even, in one part of his mind – the rational part? the conscious part? – whether he had done anything at all. But he must have done something and buried the result, for the floorboards were arching slightly and that meant the corpse's stomach had not been pierced. In the gut there had set in chemical reactions and the ballooning digestive gases were pressing against the boards, causing them to expand.

He thought vaguely of exhumation: digging up the rubbery, sticky, stinking mass, cutting it up with garden shears, then incinerating it. It would be a miracle if he were not caught. But now, inexplicably, in another part of his mind there was guilt. How could he atone? Attend the funerals of total strangers? He could see himself bowing his head among the roses and the words of the beautiful solemn sermon, knowing that, below, human tissue was becoming slowly indistinguishable from diarrhoea.

6

Above him the ceiling was like the page he had left in the typewriter. Compared with the white of the moonlight it was absolutely black but compared with the darkness of the shadows it was quite pale, almost white. So he didn't know what it was. Maybe he couldn't know. Realism would claim to know but realism had its own limitations and conventions: conventions such as the knowledge that if anything apparently fantastic were to happen in a story it would all turn out to be a dream, or an illusion, or a quirk arising from a point of view: the point of view of a lunatic or an eccentric. Henry James, with his ambiguities of time and perspective, had been a master of the device, providing only the certainty that there was no room for another turn of the screw. But he *wanted* certainty! The certainty of knowing that his life, his writing had worth!

Or even knowing with certainty that they were worth nothing.

7

Kissing the swaying and turning corpse was like bobbing for apples. As soon as he moved forward to brush against his lips the cold, dry tongue, with its lingering bouquet of rotting meat, it backed away as though in black coquetry. Or perhaps he was the corpse, backing away from it. Certainly he was backing away now, for he was in the passage once more.

8

Perversely enjoying his depression, he opened the drawer and took out his letter opener. All he had to do was press the blade against his wrist and with increasing force draw it slowly back – parallel to his arm, not across it; that was a common misconception – and his life would slowly fade, like a room seen through eyes progressively more tired and filmed with sleep. All that had prevented him from slitting his wrists before was the idea that someone might walk in and revive him, leaving him with only brain damage, a staring vegetable.

Still holding the letter opener, he walked thoughtfully to the lounge. He felt a sudden, strange bond with the corpse. Why, after all, should he be spared what the previous tenant had gone through? Some pain was infinite but still had to be borne. The human mind knew no limitations in conceiving cruelty: in films, in books, even in poems. And not just the cruelty of pain, the cruelty of rope or razor, but emotional cruelty, the cruelty of the forced excision of eye belonging to wife, mother, lover, child.

And then forced defecation in the shrieking wound.

And then forced copulation with the flowing, red and ginger mass.

And then forced consumption of the decayed secretions days or even weeks later.

Etc.

He knelt, and twisted the letter-opener between two loose floorboards. They were not full-length. In fact, the floor resembled a jigsaw puzzle of different sized boards, so he was able to prise them up easily. Soon, the floor was a chessboard of wood and darkness, making him think of the grille of some oubliette.

Sick with the knowledge of what he was about to do, of what he before had not allowed himself even to imagine but now knew to be unavoidable, he removed the cord from his dressing-gown, formed a crude noose, attached the other end of the cord to the steel light-fitting, placed the noose around his neck.

And paused.

9

From the crate he saw that he had taken two books: one by O. Henry, the title page of which was illuminated, and one by Beckett: *Stories and Texts for Nothing*. Both smelt of mould and had been attacked by silverfish.

He wondered why silverfish were considered to be silver. They were really only grey, that is, black or white. Only mirrors were silver. Until one stood in front of them, of course, and then they were nothing at all. He went into his room, sat in his chair, and closed his eyes.

Semi-Detached

1

As far as Eddy could see, the presence – if there was one – had left no definite trace. Nevertheless, he glanced around the lounge again. Cement was visible in the corners where flakes of plaster, like pages from some tiny, ancient book, had come away. The house was old, having been built in the convict days. The window-panes were thicker at the bases than at the tops, and were far too high to be cleaned easily. The exposed beams, the grey of an old man's hair, were reputed to have come from a shipwreck. Strangely for Australia the house was semi-detached.

Telling himself the whole idea of a presence was absurd, he poured himself a mug of Horlicks, pushed aside his worn copy of *Dissemination* and wondered when Rita would get home. Lately, her behaviour had become increasingly aberrant. On the one hand, she was spending more and more time away from him, while on the other, she was lavishing on him, when present, attentions and kindnesses surpassing those even from the early days of their relationship. He could understand in a way her spending more time away from him: they didn't have much in common and it was only fair that she should be able to go to amusement parks and bars with her new friends while he stayed at home and read Idealist philosophy. But it was hard to avoid the conclusion that eventually she would be seeking to give him the moon but have no time in which to do it.

He jumped as the door slammed.

"Eddy? Oh, I've missed you!" Arms spread wide, Rita – twenty-four years old, little beak-like nose, hair like red fairy floss – flung herself on him, nestled against him. "You're so nice to understand me."

"It's nothing." He gently detached her arms so that he might examine the expression on her face. "Did you go on many rides?"

"Yes! The Flying Chairs, the Wheel of Death, the Dive Bomber. It was fantastic. Then we went to a club and shouted each other these unreal slammers and shooters…"

"I feel guilty about not going with you."

"Oh don't be. We still do lots of things together."

"Well, actually we don't, lately. Maybe I should at least meet these new friends of yours. I promise I won't embarrass you."

"I know you won't. But let's just wait a little. It's hard to say what I mean." She glanced around the room. "What have you been up to while I was gone?"

"Let's see. That was two days ago, wasn't it?" he asked pointedly. Despite Rita's affection he couldn't help feeling slighted and hurt that a relationship that had begun with their spending every moment together had now reached the stage where more than twenty-four hours could pass without his seeing her. She phoned regularly but the spoken word was no substitute for her being present. Oddly, while she herself was now nothing like the person he had first met (there was a four-year gap between them), her phone calls were exactly the same in content and in tone as they had always been. It was as though each call were a communication with the past, with some distant origin. The whole situation was making him feel increasingly unreal. "I started my new paper on textual theory, 'Universal Intersemioticity, Barthes, and Derrida: Death of the Author or Death of the Reader?'. It's related to my earlier one on Heidegger's 'The House of Being'. That's about all. Just mooning about, really. Oh, and I listened to that Haydn Duets CD you bought me. The one you bought at the same time as your Abba CD. What was it called again - *Aberrations*?" He tried to smile.

She went into the kitchen. "I have a really stellar meal planned for you tomorrow, so that you have something nice while I'm out. You're not allowed to look in these bags to spoil the surprise."

"It's going to be Steak Tartare, isn't it? I was only talking about it the other day. And you're a fantastic cook."

"Well, you'll just have to wait and see." She tried to maintain an air of secrecy but it was clear to him that he had guessed the surprise.

He changed the subject. "About the only thing of real interest that happened was that today I felt convinced there was some sort of a presence in the house. Although perhaps 'presence' is the wrong word."

She gave him a sidelong glance. "Well, this house often gives me the creeps." She went back into the lounge and threw herself on the settee. "What happened?"

Forced to follow her to continue the conversation without shouting, he shrugged. "It's hard to be sure. I felt as though my every movement and thought were being contemplated and analysed." He glanced at himself in the mirror and made a mental note that after he next washed his hair he would have to look at the spots where the red dye was fading. "Not only that, I felt as though various elements of the room were being contemplated and analysed, too. The holes in the plaster, the exposed beams. As though someone were trying to determine their significance."

"Did you feel like you were in danger? You did, didn't you? I can read you like a book. According to folklore they used to send canaries down mineshafts."

"It was probably just my imagination. Altered states of mind commonly accompany long spells of isolation."

"Having a dig at me again for spending time with my friends?"

"Good God, no," he replied quickly. Rita's temperament could switch from loving effusion to spirited tartness in a fraction of a second. "It was in Jung, I think." He glanced at the antique wall-clock. The Roman numeral V on its dial reminded him, as always, of an omission sign. "Anyway, I only waited up so that I could see you. I'm tired. I think I'll go to bed."

"OK. I've got a lot of TV programmes to catch up with. I'll see you in the morning."

He kissed her absently and went to his bedroom.

2

He woke several hours later. He was being contemplated. He was sure of it! He sat up, and peered into the dark. The shadows seemed to be reeling, as if they were about to be drawn into some vortex. But he told himself that this could be an illusion created by blood rushing from his head. He massaged his temples.

Suddenly, the movement of the shadows stopped, but the feeling that there was a presence remained. There was an examining, a probing of him – and also a sense of imminence. Whatever was there was curious as to what he would do next, and still wasn't sure what he stood for.

He climbed out of bed and turned on the light. "Rita, could you come here, please?"

There was a sound from down the passage. Clearly she was still watching TV. "What is it?"

"The feeling of a presence. It's here again."

"Hang on a second. I'll be right with you."

The door opened, and there appeared the familiar shock of red hair contrasting so strikingly with nacreous skin. She paused, as though to take in the lie of the land. "Yes, you're right," she said at last. "This is wicked! Maybe the house is built on an old graveyard. In places, the floor isn't quite level. Perhaps there's an elemental." She faced him. "Did I tell you what CB said to me on the dodgems today? I think he's got a crush on me…"

"How does it strike you, the presence?"

She forced herself to concentrate. "The feeling is most pronounced towards you. Has it communicated at all? You know, aloud." She moved closer. "It's a presence but around you there's a kind of lack!"

He smiled dryly. "Yes, I'm sure you know a lot about lacks. You and it must have a lot in common!"

"Well, if you're going to be shitty I'm going back to the TV." She stalked away.

Put out, he sat on the bed. "Behaving true to type, I see!" he called, and then regretted it. But it was too late. The door was slammed shut and Rita was gone – if she had ever been there…

Moreover, the presence too seemed to have gone. Was it temporarily sated? If Rita was right, and it had turned him into a lack, maybe the total result was now a neutrality. Suddenly overwhelmingly weary, he went back to bed.

3

In the morning, a scrawled note from Rita greeted him, telling him in gilt ink that she had gone out and didn't know when she'd be back. As usual it was covered with 'X's and love-hearts and allusions to expensive presents when she returned.

He closed his eyes, suddenly trying to picture her. The red hair, of course... The beak-like nose and nacreous skin... But really, he couldn't say more than that. Was he concerned? He allowed himself to fall into the settee, trying to focus. But her physical details still wouldn't link up and some he couldn't remember ever having known. While, for example, he could picture her slender waist – she was very vain about that – he couldn't picture her arms or her back. So was she now characterised not only by physical but also by mental absence? Presumably in her social circle she was still just as real, but clearly, sadly, he was unlikely to have any experience of that any time soon, or ever...

He took up her note and a pen and began to doodle. Soon, each 'X' was part of a word. He found that he had written 'exit', 'exist', 'exergue'. The love-hearts he simply rounded, so that they became backsides.

Suddenly, he burst into tears, all the months of pretending to himself that he wasn't being taken for a ride, that nothing was amiss with their relationship, finally crushing him. The pain was far worse than if she had simply walked out. Surely breaking up with someone should be against the law, like any other action that produced injury? What did she see in such common, vacuous, childish people? How could she love him and them at the same time? Did it mean that he and they were in the same category? They'd consider him a 'creep'. He knew the type. He tried to imagine her talking to them but the faces were blank and the words mere detached syllables. Losing control, he screamed as loud as he could, longing to strain his vocal cords, longing to give himself pain that was at least physical in origin.

And then he stopped. He had felt the presence again – far stronger than before, as if it had gained something.

Feeling as though he were on a roller coaster, he shook his head, tried to concentrate on Rita. Absently, he went to the kettle and went through the motions of making a cup of tea. He would have to resolve things, regain his peace. He would march over to Rita's friends' places – he had secretly written down all their addresses and other personal details – and demand that they release her back to him. Surely they would be sensible. Or would they simply defer to Rita, allow her to make the decision? If so, and she chose not to spend more time with him, he would do something extreme: beat her, perhaps, give her a good hiding. And to get his own back on her friends he would break into their homes when they were at work, conceal drugs – 'mull', they would call it – beneath the floorboards with suspicious amounts of money, then tell the police anonymously.

But where would he get the drugs? And did Rita have keys he could secretly copy? He realised he didn't know. He had never inquired.

The feeling of a presence was intense.

He collapsed into a corner. Simultaneously with the intense feeling of presence he himself felt a mere nothing. He strove to rekindle his anger, strove to recall examples of Rita's superficiality, her unintentional meanness. But he couldn't. And it wasn't fair that he couldn't. The presence must have stolen from him!

He considered the idea that he and the presence therefore had something in common. The notion seemed unavoidable. But if that was right, the implication was that the presence must also contain within itself a certain lack. It must to a certain extent also be in a half-and-half state, permanently.

To his surprise, he realised he no longer felt so weak. And with this realisation, he felt stronger still. It was as though his learning he was on a par with the presence had turned him suddenly into some animal – a bird of prey perhaps – which, though injured, has devoured and may well recover and grow to be invincible.

He went to the knife drawer. He had apparently weakened one opponent with a philosophical argument, a mental duel. He would weaken – no, kill! – the other with a knife. Such a time of contrast would provide the ideal opportunity. He pictured Rita (or was that 'Reader', he wondered, thinking of his paper), with red lines criss-crossing her white throat, scrawls of blood vandalising the text that was their spoilt, shared life. Rita with a plurality of lips from which to gush.

There would be intense pain, of course: physical pain for her and the accompanying and subsequent mental pain for him. And screaming. Wonderful, real, presence-affirming screaming. On the other hand, his dominance might be achieved strategically by simply strengthening and tightening to the point of painfulness the bonds of their relationship, so that for her there was no play, no give. Maybe they would have children. He could easily stop using protection without her knowing and then tie her up for weeks or even months if she wanted an abortion. Disseminate his seed, write her sentence in stretch-marks. He replaced the knife but only half-closed the drawer.

He would have to see.

Your Pain is My Pain

1

"You could still change your mind if you wanted to." Dan glances with grim satisfaction first at the sign reading 'Dr Wright – Counsellor' and then at Lance's worried expression. "One call to Virgin Blue and you're on your way to another state."

"No, far be it from me to stand in the way of the law. God forbid that I should actually be happy."

"But that's the very point. No one has the right to be happy if they're causing pain to someone else in the process. No one at all." The vehemence of Dan's words is such that several people in the waiting room look up startled from their magazines. He resumes, in a quieter voice, "If you say otherwise you might just as well condone domestic violence, war, or use of the rack or drawing and quartering."

"Well, I love Nicholas and Peter and nothing any counsellor can say will alter that. I'm sorry I hurt you after six years and I still love you but I'm not *in* love with you." He stares defiantly back at Dan. His eyes, the colour of evening clouds, are fixed and sharp.

"Whatever, shortly we are going to sign a legally-binding contract agreeing to a mutual pain-minimisation strategy. You'll just have to resign yourself to that and not be childish."

"Maybe, just maybe, one outcome of this contract will be that you learn to see why I love Nicholas and Peter."

At this, Dan grimaces, wondering what a man so devastatingly beautiful at eighteen and no less appealing at twenty-four can see in two such stereotypes. Nicholas: an out-of-condition boutique manager, interested in clubbing, achieving a 'six-pack' and enthusiastic about the soundtrack to *The King and I*. Peter: a weather-beaten worker in the hospitality industry, interested in clubbing, achieving a 'six-pack' and enthusiastic about the soundtrack to *The King and I*. He feels an absolute revulsion for the pair; an infinite repugnance for their meanness in stealing Lance from him. If only he could make them suffer the pain he has suffered! He tells himself that he'd like to strangle them; break their arms and legs – anything to make them experience what he has gone through.

Thank God, he thinks, Lance will soon be compelled by law to spend some time with him, with the option of paying for independent 'sincerity monitoring' if they choose. Thank God for a compassionate society that appreciates just how crushing separations can be and how people have a right for the resulting pain to be minimised.

"Mr Richmond and Mr King?" A gangling man appears at the door. He is in early middle age with greying whiskers shaved in the shape of bent knees. His black eyes are set rather too close together and a mop of dark, thick, kinked hair covers his head. He glances at them.

"Reporting for duty," Dan says in a jovial tone that bears no relation to his mood.

"Please take a seat. I'm Dr Wright, as you no doubt know." He bustles about, apparently hunting for a document. "And you, Mr King, have a distinguished name. Did you know it was a Daniel King who first came up with the revolutionary idea that society must protect its citizens from the pain of relationship-breakups? That it owes a duty of care to them?"

"No, I didn't. I'm a freelance writer, not a historian." He lies back in one of the two plastic maroon chairs that face Dr Wright's desk and gives Lance, who has settled uneasily into his, a sidelong glance. "But I'm infinitely relieved that he did."

"I expect you are. Now, I know the basic details of your circumstances but in my experience a good first step is for the two parties to provide the details in their own words. So?"

Dan makes a generous gesture to Lance. "Over to you, Lance."

Lance shoots a suspicious, bitter glance at him, and then appears to steel himself. "There's not much to relate, really. I love Dan but I'm not *in* love with him. I met these two guys who are really great fun. It started as a crush but now I just want to spend all my time with them."

Dr Wright says, "Well, under the pain-minimisation laws and mental health act, Lance, you won't be allowed to spend *all* your time with them. That would cause Dan pain, yes?" He glances at Dan. "It's like child-access. There has to be balance. Unless... no, no, we'll leave that on one side that for a moment. Go on."

"I might have known the system would be weighted against me." Lance stares at the ceiling, folds his arms, makes his voice sound bored. He fiddles with his blond-tipped, close-cropped hair (which always makes Dan think of summer straw). "Nicholas, Peter and I are really close. We all wear these rings." He holds up his index finger, displaying a narrow band of parti-coloured metal. "The three strands stand for us. I bought them on the web."

Dr Wright leans back in his chair and throws his pen in the air, which he promptly fails to catch. "The file mentioned trinogamy but I wanted to be sure. A move to something... *unconventional* like a three-way relationship may be symptomatic of a more deep-seated problem but that's a risk we may want to take when we proceed." He steeples his fingers and takes a deep breath. "Look, there's been a recent advance that may be more satisfying emotionally to both of you than a mere contract could ever be. Are you interested?"

"Yes," says Lance.

"Go on," says Dan.

"Quite simply, it's a drug. A safe one, I emphasise, with no side-effects, although I'll need a blood sample from both of you to see just what's coursing round your veins. You see, the brain is a vast chemical factory. When we're in love certain chemicals are secreted that are present at no other time. And a similar thing happens, only with different chemicals, when we experience pain. What this drug – which is called Meme, incidentally – will do is allow you, Lance, to experience a bit of what Dan is experiencing, and you, Dan, to experience a bit of what Lance is experiencing. Then it will be over to you. A weight off both your minds."

"We'll take it," Lance says triumphantly.

2

As the door slams and the sound of rapid footsteps dies away, Dan wonders if the Meme really will work. They took their first dose only half an hour ago but, apart from a residual sweetness around his lips, he feels no different. He experiences relief in the knowledge that if the drug doesn't work the pain-minimisation contract will still be an option for them. But whatever happens in the future, he tells himself, the door has still been slammed *now* and Lance is not only on the other side of it but also increasingly far from him, on his way to Peter and Nicholas – or, as he calls them, 'Dr Jerkoff and Mrs Hyde'.

He paces around the table, dejectedly noting the set of tumblers Lance bought him on their second anniversary. They are of cut glass, the angular trenches making him think of claw marks or broken window panes. He checks himself. He shouldn't think of aggression. He has to give the Meme time to work. The drug could be the solution to everything for them. That's always been his problem, really: aggressiveness, anger and – he's ashamed to admit it – actual violence. Lance's behaviour has been unpardonable, there's no doubt about that, but perhaps if he'd controlled his anger sometimes he might have been able to win him over. Well, he won't be angry now. He'll be relaxed and listen to music.

He allows himself to fall into the blue felt-covered divan, trying to decide what music would be appropriate, what music might relax him. He usually listens to classical music, by composers such as Liszt and Wagner, but he feels that in his current state he can't face anything so intense. He wants something cheerful, something uplifting – certainly not a *Te Deum*. But he doesn't own any light classical music, if such a thing even exists.

Absently, he runs a hand through his blond beard and hair and finds his eyes coming to rest on Lance's collection of Culture Club CDs.

3

Carefully (so as to give himself time to ask yet again whether he's doing the right thing) Dan parks his Statesman in the drive outside Peter and Nicholas's house. The driveway, which is as steep as a Nazi salute, is strewn with gum leaves. Then he peers at the house. Weatherboard, it looks run-down, especially in the late afternoon sun. Paradoxically, it gives the impression it could have been built yesterday, with split levels, recesses and projections of obscure function; he recalls he has often disparaged the house to Lance as a cross between a church and an abattoir.

He looks about for Lance's green Sigma and sees that it is parked farther down the drive than usual. As he gets out of his vehicle, he also sees that Lance is hurrying along the path towards him.

"Well, you were right, of course. I don't know how they ever appealed to me. I'll make it up to you somehow." He flings his arms around him.

"Oh!" Taken aback at such an about-face in less than twenty-four hours, Dan gently detaches Lance's arms so that he may examine the expression on his face. "Are you sure? That's fantastic but I suppose it's the effect of the Meme. Can you remember whether Wright said the effects are permanent or not?"

"It doesn't matter. This is real. I'll cook you a really nice steak tomorrow as a first step towards making up."

"I hope you were courteous to Nicholas and Peter."

"*What*?" Lance's eyes are wide and then he nods knowingly. "Oh, I'm with you now. You have my attitudes and I have yours. Well, that's a bit pathetic, isn't it? The overall effect is no alteration. Surely this could have been anticipated?"

At that moment an imposing figure and a shorter one with a head bald like a monitor lizard's appear at the doorway and move towards them in a kind of synchronised, calculated gait: Nicholas and Peter.

"I suppose you've come here triumphant that you've won after all." Peter looks Dan up and down.

Dan makes an embarrassed gesture. "What? No, actually I've come to make things up! I've lacked compassion and understanding with regard to Lance's attraction to you, and that wasn't right."

"God, listen to him," Peter says to Nicholas. "Does he expect us to believe this bull? Aggression alternating with sheer tedium. That's you all over, you prick."

Nicholas snickers, and nods.

Lance says, "How dare you speak to Dan like that! He was my love while you two were screwing your way through every piece of night club trash you could get your hands on!"

"Easy, Lance." Dan puts a restraining hand on Lance's arm, and then faces Nicholas and Peter. "You two have caused us pain and are continuing to do so. I feel disappointed, because I have a genuine empathy for you now. But we know what to do under these circumstances."

"Right," Lance states drily. "Spelt W-R-I-G-H-T." He steps up to Peter and punches him in the solar plexus, pauses, and then gives his left temple a glancing blow. Peter is so taken aback that he just stands there, trying not to reel backwards. By the time that Lance has thrown him to the ground, however, he is gasping and Dan is gently drawing his lover backwards and towards his car.

4

"That's right; Meme works but in many cases its effect will be lessened because no couple is isolated but is part of a web of social interactions that spans the whole community; Peter and Nicholas need the drug, yes, but I know that Nicholas is also having several flings that Peter doesn't know about; one is with a guy on the net whose nick is Zircon – God knows there must be more." Lance says all this in one breath and then folds his arms, challenging Dr Wright to speak.

Dan muses, "The ideal solution would be to pour massive quantities of the drug into the dams. Then everyone would feel compelled to be nice to one another, not behave like something out of the middle ages. But we'd need a blood sample from everyone, wouldn't we?"

Dr Wright is attempting to balance a pen against his paper-punch. It promptly falls over and rolls on to the floor. "It's interesting that you talk about a web of social interactions, Lance, because the theorist I was telling you about on your first visit said the constant play of pain and pain-minimisation strategies in our lives also forms a web – a web of differing and deferring rather like that alluded to by various poststructuralist semioticians. The pain of lack. I hope I'm not confounding you with jargon! Anyway, the idea is that this play – which links all texts to what Husserl called the 'lifeworld', blurring the distinction between them – grounds the entire human condition and its lore and is thus the responsibility of everyone. It also bears no direct relationship to conventional temporality." He shrugs. "But it's one thing to say it's the responsibility of us all, and another to say just what, beyond the current legal options, we should all do."

"Well, what did *he* say we should do? Did he consider the possibility of Meme?"

Dr Wright folds his arms. "There is no Meme. At least, not the way you think."

"*What?*" Lance stares at him. "Then what was that draught we took? And why?"

"A placebo. Sugar solution. The important thing was the *idea* and the resultant inseparable and compelling *conviction* that you would see things from each other's point of view. Once that little computer subroutine – which is what a 'meme' is, if you look the word up – entered your mental circuitry it was just a matter of hours for it to take effect and for you to be altered."

"Oh!" He sits back. "I don't know what to say. I feel like I've been made an example of. But for some reason I'm not angry about it."

Dr Wright holds his fingers in front of him, examines them as though they belonged to someone else, and then laughs urbanely. "No problem. Pain minimisation is my specialty, as you know!"

Dan says, "If what you say is right, the idea of pain-minimisation and Meme should be disseminated through the community. Think of how attitudes about women, gays, transgender issues and even whaling quickly changed. Maybe

I'll write it all down, so that others may more easily learn of it, be conditioned by it. "

"Good idea. I'd suggest a work of fiction as your vehicle. More people absorb ideas that way. They'll also experience, empathically, shock and pain, and the recuperation from them, along with the characters, linking them semiotically. By that I mean there's no absolute difference between fiction and a theoretical paper, any more than there's an absolute difference between the Dan King who's before me now and the other one I told you about who – god-like! – produced all these ideas. Everything's linked, as Whitehead pointed out."

5

Lance presses the left button on his keyring and the Sigma's door-locks rise like apathetic sentries. "Far be it from me to make predictions, but I think there's going to be a major change in the world because of experiences like ours."

Dan gets in beside Lance. "I pray you're right. I never want to go through the last weeks again." He laughs. "When we get home I suggest a nice sweet tumbler of cordial!"

"Cordial? That's a bit bland, isn't it?"

"Blandness may be what we have to get used to. If we reduce all the emotional peaks in life, there won't be much left. Still, anything is better than pain."

"Agreed." Lance smiles weakly, and kisses him.

Dan smiles, not exactly discontented, but aware that there is something just beyond his conscious grasp that he ought to know. He shrugs. There will be plenty of time to mull it over later, if he can find the enthusiasm.

Heaven and/or Hell

1

"So what was the news with my Message?" Emma lowers herself on to the couch and closes her eyes. Then she looks up at Ray.

"It's nothing you don't already know. It was all I could find out at this stage. You'll be going to either Heaven or Hell."

"There must have been more than that!"

Ray shrugs. "They said you'll find out which at the appropriate point." He also sits on the couch. "Don't worry about it. It's the same for everyone."

Emma clicks in exasperation. "That's puerile reasoning. If you were told you were going to be cast into, say, some metal-worker's forge tomorrow, it wouldn't make things better knowing that other people were going to be as well." She directs him a pointed expression. "Just ask those who were put into – what was it you kept talking about that time? – Moloch."

"A forge?" Ray makes a wry expression and runs a hand through his hair, which Emma always says is like rusted steel wool and should be shaved off. "Well, in a sense that might be half of humanity's exact fate. There's probably not much difference between being in a forge and being in the lake of fire that is supposed to make up Hell."

"Oh God." Shaking, Emma lifts herself from the couch and goes to the window. The agapanthus blooms, like mauve exploding fireworks, are silhouetted against the dusk sky and its dark pine trees. "I'd try to find out for myself if it weren't for the fact that the whole Message idea is so suspenseful, so shocking. God knows I can't ask my children to do that sort of thing. They won't even speak to me!"

"You are aware, aren't you, that it's possible to make a Message less of a shock?"

"How do you mean?" She half-turns.

"Well, given how stressful it is, with the Message saying whether you're going to Heaven or Hell and so on, you can arrange for it to blend into the background, so to speak."

"I'm not with you."

"Just imagine you were anxious about the sound of, say, a particular bell. One way of reducing the anxiety would be to provide yourself with a background of bell sounds. Then the stressful bell sound wouldn't stand out so much when it eventually arrived." He laughs. "If the medium really is the message, and you don't like the message, change the medium!"

"All right." Emma narrows her lips. "Tell me how my Heaven or Hell Message is going to arrive, and you can provide a similar background. Near duplicates of the Message, or whatever." She shakes her head. "Under the circumstances it's the least you can do for me."

"According to my source, the Message has a good chance of arriving as a letter in the mailbox."

2

The following day Emma listens anxiously for the postman. She doesn't know if Ray has had time to provide his 'background' yet. She imagines the relief of finding in the letterbox just great wads of advertising material: fliers and circulars and the peculiar bicolour notices from real estate agents and other nonsense she usually detests. There is something reassuring about such texts now, she thinks. And all texts, all words – according to know-it-all Ray, anyway – are characterised by lack (or 'lacunae' as he puts it); so if the content of a text is nonsense, the lack, presumably, will negate it into something worthwhile. She feels unsure. Tries to remember whether they had discussed such things in her night school literature class.

And then, surrounded by a pall of dust from the dry headland road, there draws near the familiar figure of the motorcycle-riding postman, his bags of letters like the pollensacs of some desert bee. She watches as he withdraws some papery rectangles from the left bag and stuffs them in the letterbox.

As she slowly makes her way down the path, she wonders for what seems the thousandth time exactly why there has to be a Heaven or Hell Message. No one even knows how the content of the Messages is decided, by whom, or what its ultimate source is. All that is known is that the recipient is given a clear pointer with regard to Heaven or Hell some time after turning seventy, if not before. Surely, she tells herself, some ambiguous book – a book that anyone can interpret in an unlimited number of ways, and where 'seems' is more important than 'is' – would be preferable. A black-and-white Message is so blunt, so mean, even to someone, such as she, who was born in a slum and therefore familiar with suffering. So resistant to ambiguity. Again she feels unsure.

The first letter is an application/invitation from a credit card company. Absently, she puts it in her pocket. The second letter, however, is just a folded piece of paper. Full of apprehension, she opens it:

EMMA ANDERSON IS GOING TO HEAVEN

Emma feels as though she's going to faint. She grasps the letterbox, nearly tearing her mauve slacks on the fence. She's going to Heaven. She can't credit it! Not Hell! How can her mind contain such relief?

But does that mean she is going to die, soon? No, she remembers that the Messages never provide any indications as to time. Besides, Heaven must surely be incompatible with any future unpleasantness. So perhaps she will experience Assumption into Heaven without dying, like the Blessed Virgin.

There are more letters and four more pieces of paper. Clearly, then, Ray did have time to arrange the background! Scrabbling the letters open, she sees that they all duplicate the first Message:

EMMA ANDERSON IS GOING TO HEAVEN
EMMA ANDERSON IS GOING TO HEAVEN
EMMA ANDERSON IS GOING TO HEAVEN
EMMA ANDERSON IS GOING TO HEAVEN

Suddenly, she feels a ghastly doubt. Could *all* the Messages be Ray's creation? The real Message may not have arrived yet. She hurries inside.

Ray is making toffee apples. He puts down a paring-knife and licks his fingers as she enters. Beams. "How was the post?"

"Ray, please tell me that you had a word with the postman, got him to show you my Message and then made copies of it before they ended up in the letterbox. Please, please tell me that."

He shrugs. "It's as you say. I provided exactly four Messages. I thought it would be nicer to have them all duplicate the real one, just in case you thought a made-up 'You are going to Hell' Message was legitimate."

"You are telling the truth? You wouldn't lie to me, would you? I mean to spare me anxiety."

"Of course not." He places a toffee apple on top of the blender, making a sugary ring. "Think about it, Emma. Why should you go to Hell? Apart from that sharp tongue of yours, which always seems to put people in shops offside, you've never done anything wrong. On the contrary, you do everything right! You give your embroidery and knitting to charity. You're kind to animals. In a word, you're definite Heaven material!"

Emma bites her lip and shakes her head. Her dyed-auburn, kinked, mannish hair barely changes position. "I just wish I knew what Hell really meant."

"Is that what concerns you?" He stares at a crack in the ceiling, his hands toying with the 'v' of the stretched and archaic woolen jumper she detests (even though she had knitted it for him). "Well, let's look at the matter objectively. It would be a state of almost absolute lack, with just enough of a trace of presence for you to be aware of that lack. And the state would always be 'there', like a story in a book – although reality itself is like a book, in my opinion, as all texts blend into one another. Plays, newspapers ... and all the stuff about everlasting fire and red hot pokers is nonsense. Fire is too much of a presence. The pain it gave would be so excruciating the finite human brain wouldn't be able to reflect on it for more than a thousandth of a second. Did you know that Lucifer is supposed to have wings?"

"So what would Heaven be?"

"Who can say? The opposite of the above, presumably. But maybe they would be the same. Whatever that means."

"In any case, I can relax now." In sudden transports, she grasps his hands, as if to do a waltz. "Let the belle of the ball take her youthful-looking fifty year-old literature professor to bed and do something heavenly!"

3

That night, however, Emma can't sleep. She keeps remembering her past transgressions: the times she's cheated at draughts; the times she's spent too much money at sideshows. She wonders how those deeds can be reconciled with her going to Heaven. Surely such transgressions can't just be overlooked? It would make a mockery of ethics. But the Messages never allude to a middle ground between Heaven and Hell, so she has to be bound for one or the other.

She turns to contemplate Ray, spread-eagled beside her. She asks herself if she really can believe him. So much depends on his telling the truth about the Messages. He must have told lies at some stage in his life. It's impossible for anyone not to. And just suppose the Message had been to tell her she was going to Hell. Ray would have spared her that. As he implied earlier, he would be too nice to do otherwise.

She realises with a sudden dismay that her fate is just as uncertain as it was before.

Feeling as though she's all at once a figure in a report of some highly unreliable and sensational newspaper, her whole life open to unseemly contemplation and criticism, she gets out of bed, deciding to study the Messages again. For when the stakes are infinite, she realises, even a slight doubt becomes magnified into something overwhelming. The only chance is to see if there could be some faint distinction among the slips of paper that will enable her to tell Ray's Messages from the legitimate one – assuming there is a legitimate one.

In the moonlight through the bay windows the Messages appear ghostly and slightly unreal. Reluctant to turn on the light and wake Ray, she peers at the paper of each in turn. There are darker coarse shreds, like random characters of some unknown alphabet, but nothing to tell the pieces of paper apart. She holds them to her nose. They have no particular scent.

If only she could get to the truth! But how is that to be done with texts? They withhold so much. No, they withhold everything! Suddenly incensed, she screws the Messages into a ball, the knowledge of her lack of information unbearably painful to her.

4

Over the next few days, Emma has increasing difficulty controlling her anxiety. "It's all right for you, you fucking prick!" she screams at Ray. "At least if I knew I was going to Hell it would be definite. But this lack of certainty! I can't bear it! We're not just talking about days!"

"For the thousandth time, Emma, there is no uncertainty. The Message I duplicated was clear. You are going to Heaven. Relax by listening to some of your popular classics like that Liszt symphony. Or some of Bernstein's Schumann cycle. You've always followed him closely."

She lunges forwards and grasps his neck with both hands, stares into his eyes, teeth bared. "But how can I get to the truth behind your eyes? *You could be lying!*"

"I'm not lying! You're choking me!"

"And that could be a lie, too!" She releases him and runs her fingers back and forth violently in her scalp, as if trying to make it bleed. "This lack... it couldn't be worse if we didn't even know if there was a Heaven or a Hell!" She leans close. "Answer one thing, Ray. Have you ever told a lie?"

Ray shifts uncomfortably, plays with the seam of his dun corduroy pants. "Well, I suppose I must have done, at some point. But not over anything significant like this."

Emma picks up the paring-knife, still sticky on the sideboard. "Swear on pain of death that you have never lied. I won't be satisfied with anything less!"

"Emma, don't be silly. You know I can't swear that."

Emma stabs him in the right eye.

5

It is three o'clock in the morning. Or is it five o'clock in the afternoon? Emma realises she doesn't know. She can't know.

Could it be she's only injured Ray? She buries her head in the eiderdown, hoping it will suffocate her. She can't steel herself to go into the lounge and see, but she has a horrible, unbearable certainty that he's dead.

The conclusion is obvious. Not only is she not going to Heaven, she is actually going to Hell, has always been going to Hell and is in fact in Hell now. The Message about her going to Heaven had been designed to make the contrast greater, more poignant, so that she would suffer more. She wonders if there should be grim satisfaction in knowing that Ray therefore was lying after all. There is no grim satisfaction. Just an infinite, unbearable, empty horror.

Beside her bed is a folded newspaper. She can just see some sensational headline about a plot involving the heir to a fortune. The plot ended in suicide. She flings the newspaper on to the floor. But even when it is out of sight she knows that the story is still there.

Martial Arts

1

Coria opens the front door, snakes off her white belt, and throws it on to the couch. Then she smiles at Dan, who is doing the splits on the hall-runner. "Well, that was my first Taekwondo class. And I must say it was fantastic. I should have enrolled years ago."

Nodding in approval, Dan slowly brings his legs together and bows in mock formality to his reflection in the window. The image of his aquiline profile, with its Number 1 haircut and brow like a bluff overlooking some abyss, breaks up as it shifts, the pattern of light. "I knew you would enjoy it. What did you learn?"

"Well, the initial workout contained nothing surprising. Mostly squats and an excruciating thing called the 'duck walk'. But then I was taught some stretch exercises, the horse stance, and the front snap kick. Mr Kong, my instructor, was impressed."

Resolutely, Dan adopts a fighting stance. "Just consider… in four years you'll be a black belt, like me." He looks over his shoulder and aims a back kick at a pile of linen that Coria left on the coffee table earlier. "For now, we'll just have to be content to be black and white. Around brown is when it gets hard. *Gup yuhl...* well, it's a start."

"You'll?" Coria plumps herself on to the couch, the arms of which resemble clenched fists, and vaguely makes her 'I want a Fanta' gesture. "So what have you been doing? Working on a new story I suppose?" She grimaces.

"You really should try to be more sympathetic towards my writing. I know it doesn't grab you but it really is impressive, though I do say so myself – vast reservoirs of meaning. At least approach it with an open mind." He points towards the fridge. "And yes, your deciding to learn martial arts made me want to write a story on the same subject. But beyond the title and a few sentences I haven't progressed very far. I may show you later." He makes a stern expression. "If you behave."

These last words register with Coria; she pretends to groan. "Oh D. No discipline today. I'm too tired after my class."

"You know the rule, Coria. Any slackness with regard to household obligations leads to punishment. The linen that was on the table should have been put tidily away hours ago. And the cushions on the couch are not aligned."

He studies Coria. A round, rather plain woman with buff hair that is kinked and parted away from a somewhat indeterminate, slightly drawn face, she always enjoys the verbal duelling that precedes their love-making. Presumably working as a receptionist makes any diversion welcome. Not for the first time he tries to remember exactly when they had decided to introduce B and D into their relationship. Both of them enjoy it – it may even have stopped them from splitting up – but he can remember a time when the idea of pain would have nauseated Coria. They have been married ten years, however, and experience has taught him that trying to locate crucial moments is pointless; they are strewn through the years like the linen on the floor.

"You are right, Dan. I must be disciplined."

"Bend over the couch while I fetch the horse-whip."

Coria does so. She sneaks a grin at him, before adopting her usual repentant expression. "I love it when you have to *fetch* the horse-whip. It makes it all like a rite. I blame your Scottish background. Or maybe working as a bank-teller makes you assertive."

Dan allows his expression to relax. "If you like rites you're going to love the Taekwondo *poomse* you'll be learning at the class. With the 'Basic Pattern', as you do the movements you trace out the initial 'I'. And some have a symbolic, almost other-worldly significance. Warriors across the sea, and to other worlds.... "

'Martial Arts', by Dan King.

On the grassy hilltop. The ten giant gas tanks. Great reflective rectangles, reveling in their separateness. Dan cranes up at the one closest to him. It is narrower than the rest and bears the vermilion and red emblem of Shell. Like the others, though, it has a helical ladder, reaching from the grass-banks to the sky.

He wonders why he is so drawn to these massive reservoirs. Perhaps the fact that he visited them first in the very earliest days of his childhood has given them a primeval, mysterious appeal. Discrete, those memories. Like the tanks. He can still see himself wandering barefoot among them, being told by his parents that when he is in England the weather will be so cold he will have to wear socks.

Could he spend the rest of his life among the tanks? He certainly wouldn't be bored if he did so. The number of different patterns of visiting the tanks sequentially is almost endless. Food, however, would be a problem. Although perhaps there are mushrooms....

"I thought you said your story was about martial arts."

Dan jumps. Coria is standing behind him.

He composes himself. "Maybe not literally. My idea was to write a story that sort of fights back against reader expectations, to show that conflict is always potentially lurking. But I'm not sure how to develop the idea. Maybe I'll have to introduce some sort of contrasting section, something so different that it shocks readers, takes them by surprise." He glances slightly disapprovingly up at her. "And please don't creep up on me when I'm reading aloud. I don't like it."

"Sorry." Coria yawns and shuffles over to his escritoire. She plumps herself on to it. "Your stuff is too arty for me, too hard to follow. I like Stephen King and Dan Brown. I remember when you tried to get me to read *Heart of Darkness*. That was a real pain." She begins to swing her legs back and forth, almost flinging off her bright vermilion rayon slippers as she does so.

"Don't you think it would be better to offer constructive comments? There's no absolute distinction between 'arty' stories and any other kind. They're all bound by constraints! And the gas tank site is real. Maybe we'll go for a spin and have a look at it. We could practise a few wrist-grabs and throws at the same time. Maybe even the round kick defence from Muay Thai, or some board-breaking. I'm accomplished at that, though I do say so myself."

"All right. I suppose I must be more deferential with regard to you now that there's a marked-out relation between us. You a black belt and me a white, I mean." She glances shyly at him. "Do you think I should call you 'sir'?"

Dan studies her with satisfied approval. "I think that would be an excellent idea." He smiles urbanely. "No time like the present – *jhoon-bee*?"

3

Dan parks his black Laser near the brow of the hill. From the carpark the gas-tanks are in profile; the squat ones remind him of sheets of paper, while the tall, thin ones are like sections of a belt. In the distance are the block-like city buildings and the question-mark of the river.

As he gets out of the Laser, he says to Coria, "I think my Martial Arts story should include lots of Korean words. To the reader unfamiliar with Taekwondo or the Korean language itself that might seem confronting or at least offputting."

"Maybe." Coria waddles up to where he is standing. "I'm no expert on stories but if the 'fighting back' elements have been planned all along, it won't be like a real attack, will it?" She gestures quickly. "Sir," she adds.

"No, but it will be like a typical martial arts session – staged. Incidentally, do you know what 'Taekwondo' actually means?"

"I know 'quando' means 'when'."

"That's in Italian! For God's sake, Coria, try to get with it." He looks her up and down critically. "And also try to lose some weight."

In spite of herself, Coria snaps, "That's a really mean thing to say – sir! Maybe you should include retorts like that in your story. Readers today would certainly be floored by such sexist put-downs."

"You're right." He sighs. "You'll have to discipline me when we get home. But for now, let's take a turn among the gas-tanks to see if they give me any ideas. After that I'll demonstrate a few take-downs that you might as well learn sooner rather than later."

They begin to walk. The air is cold, even though summer has begun. Dan glances surreptitiously at Coria, trying to determine her reaction to the experience – more specifically, to determine her level of boredom.

Hoping that conversation may defer any reporting of such feelings, he says, "As I stated in my story, one of my earliest memories is of visiting this site with my parents. It was just before our trip overseas. I wonder why the urban planners saw fit to allow gas-tanks to be placed where they would so obviously be visible. I mean, they interest me because of my memory of them, but most people would hardly consider them appealing." Again he glances surreptitiously at her. "Actually, I'll take these thoughts down for my story." He eases a pad and pen from his jeans.

"Yes, they don't do a lot for me, I must admit."

"Why does that not surprise me?" He goes up to a tank and runs his hand along a line of rivets; their impressions form an ellipsis reaching to the sky. "Oh well, let's try a few of those moves I alluded to. Or would you rather learn *Taeguek 1*?"

"It would probably be best to do the moves. The grass, which we obviously don't have at home, will provide cushioning. *Taeguek 1* I can do on the carpet. Sir."

"Actually, we'll do some one-step sparring first. Stand there." He points in front of him. "Now I'll cross my hands to the side of my head – like this – and then do a long-stance, low block. You get into the 'ready' stance. Good. *Ki-hap!*" He suddenly steps forward and lunges at Coria. Startled, she pushes him backwards and he slips, falls against a gas-tank, striking his head.

"Coria..." He feels himself fainting.

45

4

The lines of gas-tanks stretch into the distance in all directions; evenly spaced and precisely marked out, they cover each rolling, couch-covered hill and each couch-covered depression: there is no trace of city, street, vehicles, or people – or, at least, Dan can resolve none. The grass is a uniform green, except near the bases of the tanks, where it is the colour of straw.

He starts to walk. How embarrassing that he, a black-belt, should trip performing one of the most basic of all Taekwondo exercises! He shakes his head. A faint pain makes him stop. But what has happened anyway? Why are there so many gas-tanks? And where are the car and Coria?

He wipes his brow and is no less confounded to see that he is wearing his Taekwondo uniform. His black belt hangs limply, like an unraveled bandage.

There are many divisions higher than me. He wonders why these words occurred to him. He remembers they have done so before – when he was a green belt and sparring with a second-division black, some years ago. Has he been manipulated, somehow? But by whom? God, the so-called Cosmic Author? Obviously – for how else can everything have changed like this? Unless he is hallucinating. Perhaps he is some kind of apparition....

He is unconvinced. His dominant emotion, in fact, as he turns down an aisle between two particularly large gas-tanks, is the feeling that a large group of people are contemplating his behaviour at this very moment, and that not only are they surprised by what has happened to him but also they are, in some strange way he feels on the point of understanding, content.

Venerean Arts

1 Strike and Withdraw

As Daniel fell into line at the Taekwondo graduation, he narrowed his eyes, trying to spot Mimi among the ranks of waiting green-belts. He and she had split up two months ago but they still shared an interest in Taekwondo and consequently saw each other quite often. These encounters pained him greatly but the alternative – switching to a different Taekwondo venue, where he wouldn't see her – would, he knew, pain him far more. He reached into his sparring kit, withdrew a small wooden box and contemplated its contents: a Cartier brooch set with a large and striking amethyst, Mimi's birthstone. He had inherited the piece from his aunt and every time he went to the academy he tried to summon the courage to present Mimi with the little object. Sadly, he replaced it.

And then he caught sight of a familiar buff pony-tail bent into the shape of a handle: Mimi. He watched as her snub nose turned first left and then right, as it always did, as she took in her environment. He remembered her infuriating yet lovable tendency to stare at someone before collapsing into laughter at the slightest flippant remark and did a double-take when precisely this happened.

Mimi was being promoted to a striped-green this afternoon, he recalled, whereas he would be trying, probably unsuccessfully, for his red. Consequently, she would be finished and out of the Taekwondo centre before he even assumed the horse-stance. He felt a tension like a wrist-grab inside his head as he fought back tears. If only, he told himself, everyday life had the tidy, ordered quality of the martial arts! After all, martial arts were named after Mars, god of war; and one would expect life – and, especially, love – to be more, not less ordered than warfare. There should be a Venerean Arts, named after Venus, goddess of love!

Realising that intellectual activity was helping to distract his mind from its emotional burden, he pursued the idea. The fundamental martial arts action, he reflected, was the strike – a punch, a blow, or whatever – followed by a withdrawal. The idea was to produce pain. Therefore, a Venerean (not Venereal; that sounded like a disease) Arts action would be some sort of strike to produce *pleasure*, followed by withdrawal. And then, if the old 'saw' were to be believed, 'absence would make the heart grow fonder'. Suddenly quite enthusiastic, he took out his pad. Besides his interest in Taekwondo, Daniel had aspirations as a writer, and he always carried writing materials with him. Mimi had usually laughed at his lack of publishing success (and success in general; he worked as a travel agent) but he was resolved never to give up. He began to scrawl down his ideas.

"You really are determined, aren't you?"

He jumped.

Standing beside him was Mimi.

"Mimi...!" He tried to marshal his thoughts. "Is the graduation over? I thought..."

"Yes, I'm a green now, so I'm on my way home."

"But I thought you were going for your striped green!"

"That will be next. Shows how much interest you really have in me, Daniel. And you wonder why I left!"

"I have a bad memory, that's all." He felt flustered. "That's why I carry my pad. I'm not like you with your language degree. What is it now, still Spanish and Latin? I only know a few words in them: 'que' and 'vene', I mean, 'veni'." He found himself concentrating on her ears: gently curved, they were like parentheses for her head.

"That silly thing. You should use it for board-splitting practice." She laughed. "What ideas have you been jotting down this time?"

Daniel thought of what he'd been writing and suddenly was resolved. "Never mind. I have two things for you." He reached into his sparring kit and again withdrew the boxed brooch. "The first is this, given with all my love, which will never die." He tried not to feel embarrassed by the triteness of the words.

"Oh!" Taken aback, she accepted the box absently, opened it. "But I told…"

"And the second is this piece of news. You said when you left that I 'have to move on', so I'm moving to Cairns. We'll probably never see each other again." He stood. "I'm supposed to graduate today but that can wait for the Cairns Taekwondo branch. Goodbye, Mimi."

2   Take Down

As always since Mimi left, Daniel's third-storey flat felt full of emptiness. So poky, so unswept, yet so empty. Even the spaces in the most untidy room (the spare bedroom, where he kept boxes) seemed to link up and force themselves on him, remind him of permanent emptiness. Compete with the silence, the long hours. He dropped his house-key on to the glass ashtray where he dumped most small objects and closed the door. In the large mirror that hung on the side wall of the pinewood-veneer passage he barely recognised himself: his dreadlocks were sticking out like branches in all directions; his beard looked thinner than usual; and his close-set, rather hunted-looking eyes reminded him of the unlit headlights of a distant, approaching train.

He wondered if he meant what he said about Cairns. He had always wanted to move there but could he really go to a place that had so many pleasant associations of Mimi? Even the feel of wet, close air – air almost tangible, at a constant thirty degree heat – gave him a stabbing pain when he experienced it now.

Still, he reflected, he had used on her his first strategy of Venerean Arts. Maybe it would succeed, if only gradually. And if there was even a chance that it would succeed, he should be considering what the next strategy should be. He paced around the flat, pausing only to glance down at one

49

of his old Monterverdi LPs, which was rising from the floor like an A-frame house. He raised his eyebrows as he suddenly recalled its madrigal *Ogni amante è guerrier.* His flat had long been in a mess but he just had no incentive to tidy it or to clean the window panes. In his more withdrawn moments, not only when he thought of Mimi but also when he felt he'd never amount to anything, he hoped he'd fall over some object and kill himself.

Thinking of falling made him wonder whether there could be a Venerean Arts counterpart of the Martial Arts take-down or sweep. He pushed the Monteverdi sleeve idly with his foot as he turned over in his mind exactly what was involved when one took down someone. Tried to imagine one of his martial arts magazines, buried somewhere in the flat, with all their headings and diagrams. One stood before someone in the normal way, and then one suddenly performed an unexpected movement that sent the person to the floor. One took advantage of a person's expectations so that the person's relationship to the environment was completely altered. The process, if not exactly painful, certainly produced disoriented discomfort.

So a Venerean Arts take-down would be some action that suddenly, not gradually, resulted in a person's whole altered relationship with the environment: but the experience should produce not discomfort but *pleasure.*

A holiday. Mimi had always wanted to go to Sulawesi ("It's shaped just like the letter 'k'!", she often said); so he'd arrange that. Despite his promises, they hadn't been away for several years – that was probably one of the reasons for their splitting up – so an oriental holiday would be something she'd love. Not for the first time he felt infinitely relieved that she had agreed at least to remain friends with him. He couldn't remember the name of her new boyfriend, but when the latter allowed it (if she even told him), they occasionally had lunch together. Mimi could never turn down an opportunity to wolf gourmet pies and crusty rolls with herb butter at someone else's expense.

He went to the phone, dialed her number. She usually spent the time after her Taekwondo sessions 'kicking back' and sipping some exotic berry juice or wine at one of her favourite watering-holes – but there was a chance that as the Taekwondo session was a graduation rather than a workout she would have gone straight home. He found himself picturing the exuberant companions she typically collected on the other occasions, and sighed.

"Mimi LaPlante here."

"Mimi, it's Daniel. Look, I meant what I said at the academy. But I think we should mark the closure of our relationship with a really special holiday. How does nine days in Sulawesi sound?"

There was a silence. He could almost picture the range of expressions appearing, in succession, on Mimi's elliptical face: intense surprise, temptation, indecision as to whether acceptance was appropriate (or, more likely, whether she could swing it with her new boyfriend, whatever his name was), and then, finally, clinchingly, pure pleasure. Mimi had always been a hedonist, had always put herself first.

"Daniel, that's really nice." Strangely, there was a choked tone in her voice. "When? I mean, I'm away from the firm for a few weeks already, but can you reserve the tickets? Or have you already booked them? But I meant what I said about splitting up."

"I can book them without any problem, maybe on standby. Don't forget I'm a travel agent." He paused. "So you agree?"

"Well... yes! And thank you." Again, there was the choked tone.

"I'll get back to you with the flight times ASAP. We may need some shots against foreign bugs as well. I'll make a note to check."

He hung up, convinced that his Venerean Arts strategy was working. Really, he told himself, the ideas were so important they should be presented to the public – perhaps in a story, where they would pass from person to person like Dawkins' meme (he couldn't remember where he'd heard about Dawkins, but the concept had stayed close to the top of the great dump of ideas that made up his mind). Perhaps he would make the story a meta-fiction, and arrange that the reader experienced pleasure just as he did, with a happy ending....

He turned to his reflection, half-smiling at his long stick-legs (which, for all his exercise, refused to bulk up), and bowed.

3 Finish Off

Daniel wiped a cataract of sweat from his brow. The air was as close as on their holidays in Cairns but given that Mimi was beside him as they made their way through the rainforest, the feeling produced not the wrenching nostalgia he so dreaded but simple, prosaic discomfort.

"Don't get caught on these long vines," Mimi stated, carefully detaching a wiry strand from her light, butter-yellow cotton top, looking to the left and then to the right as she did so. "Their barbs will attach on anything. And they're sharp." Then she gave a little shudder of pleasure. "Ooh, I love holidays! Nothing but enjoyment and leisure for days on end!"

Daniel ran a hand through his hair which, despite the humidity, was still sticking out in all directions. "The real worry won't be thorns but getting caught up in Christian-Moslem attacks," he observed deliberately dramatically, watching her. "Affairs are supposed to have settled down a bit now, but you never know. They fight like wild animals. Green is a Moslem colour. They could hide anywhere here, ready to shoot. And Christianity is supposed to be a religion of love, of being nice to each other!"

"On the subject of green, look towards the top of that high palm. It's a birdwing butterfly! Remember the ones in Cairns, circling the trees? I wonder if it's the same species."

"How could I forget?" He stared absently at the large, soaring insect, which flashed metallic green like a Christmas tree ornament as it caught the sun. He took a sidelong glance at Mimi, dying to know what she was thinking, dying to know whether he dared to ask her how she felt about him now. So much depended on the right behaviour! His Venerean Arts strategy – which was clearly a strategy of words or even individual characters as much as actions – had worked so far but he needed some final, clinching movement to ensure that Mimi remained with him forever.

Suddenly there was a faint *whish* and simultaneously the tree in front of them had a peculiar short branch sticking out at right angles to its bark.

He opened his eyes wide, surprised. It was a knife! Alarmed, he turned, instinctively did a high block and stood in front of Mimi, embarrassed at the stagy character of the gesture.

"What are you doing?" Mimi staggered, as his closeness disoriented her, managed to right herself. "I…"

"Mimi, stay still. Someone just threw a knife at us."

"What? Oh God!" She suddenly saw the object sticking out of the tree. "Are you all right?" An expression familiar, half-forgotten, and infinitely comforting began to steal over her face.

"It missed me, fortunately," he started, when suddenly he felt a dull thud on his hand. Thinking that he had accidentally knocked it, he glanced down – and saw a knife sticking through his palm. A liquid the colour of pomegranate juice began to seep on to his sleeve. In startled detachment he realised it must be blood.

Mimi had put her arms in front of her eyes and simultaneously from the undergrowth there was a crashing sound which, surprisingly, was diminishing rather than growing in intensity. Dizzy, Daniel found himself wondering why their attacker should be running away. He reeled against a water-logged, lichen-covered tree-stump.

"Oh, you're hurt!" Mimi was beside herself. "What was I thinking of to leave you? Take deep breaths. Please don't die!" She began to cry.

Daniel could see that the flow of blood was diminishing. The knife, though responsible for the flow, was also acting as a dam to it (despite the fact that its point was projecting from the other side of his palm). In sudden, triumphant inspiration, he said, "I'll try not to, but if I do at least our last moments will be together." The cliché made him want to cringe, but he knew the effect it would have on Mimi. "Life is just one, big 'what?', Mimi."

She uttered a cry of anguish. "Oh, if you pull through we'll be together always!"

"I may not die," he said, taking slight pity on her. "And try to be collected. We're not far from the authorities. Just pretend this isn't happening, that it's not real, like a martial arts finish-off, you know, what you do when you get your opponent on the ground."

Except that it's not a finish-off of Martial Arts but of Venerean Arts, and the victim is not me but Mimi. Marveling at the good fortune of having the final strategy of Venerean Arts carried out without any effort on his part (it was almost as though someone closely aligned with him had done all the work!) he then smiled to himself. He had regained Mimi. He had succeeded.

A Dream Holiday

1

Lydia was right, Ian thought, as he stared past the escalators towards the baggage-handling area: the airport was just like a five-star hotel. It had the same sterile, white lighting; the same horde of anonymous people milling back and forth; the same arbitrary division of rest-areas into smoking and non-smoking.

So why hadn't they thought of spending their holiday in the airport before?

Idly, he tapped his suitcase, wondering when Lydia would emerge from the restroom. They had decided that at two o'clock in the morning, when (according to the display terminals) there was the greatest interval between flights, they would slip into either a male or a female restroom and spend the night there. He, of course, would first have a shower in the male restroom, while Lydia would have hers in the female; but apart from that they would not need to be separated at all.

And then Lydia emerged. He beckoned to her.

"Well? Do you think it's suitable?"

Lydia pursed her lips in a matter-of-fact manner, and nodded. "Possibly. Certainly no one should be able to see into the cubicles. Of course, the sound of flushing may be hard to sleep through."

"We could just pretend it's the noise of a hotel fountain."

"True. Remember the racket from the fountain in Malaysia? God knows why we didn't think of spending a holiday in the airport before."

55

"We'll certainly save a lot of money."

"Agreed." Lydia reached into her purse. "And the food's just as nice, too. I'd appreciate your impressions of these. I bought them when you were checking out the gents' restroom." She displayed on her palms some sky-blue fruits.

"Good lord. What is it?"

"Some kind of exotic fruit. From Queensland I think. The pulp in the middle is metallic gold in colour."

Ian broke open one of the fruits and was surprised to find that its pulp had a biscuit-like texture. He gingerly tasted it. "It's rather nice."

"Good, because I bought a few bags. They should keep us going if we get peckish in the night."

He shrugged. "So let our holiday begin! What shall we do first?"

"Go to a restaurant, I think." Lydia pointed towards a bar, where a dozen clocks showed the time in various parts of the world. "I read that when people are on holidays ten per cent of their time is spent in restaurants. I've heard good reports about that one, too. It's Malaysian."

"Right! I'll get a baggage locker and then some wine from the duty-free." He kissed her. "That brand of wine with the Monet label."

2

"I've eaten too much." Ian patted his stomach and then lowered himself into a chair beneath a display terminal. He looked up at his wife. "Any ideas now?"

"I think we should take in the sights." She gestured in the direction of a group of tropical palms. "Those, for example. They really are very fine shrubs. Easily comparable to any we saw when we were actually in Malaysia." She started in the direction of the palms.

"You're right, of course." He hurried to catch up with her. "I wouldn't be surprised if they were of exactly the same genus."

Arriving at the first palm, Lydia looked it up and down approvingly. "That's so impressive. Just think of the diseases to which it would be subject in the tropics. Insects, too, like cicadas. We're seeing it at its best here."

"It's certainly very fine." The palm reminded Ian of a green fountain. He reached to grasp the tip of one of its leaves. "Cool and green, like flowing water. And look at the one on its right. I've never seen such an exquisite orchid!"

"Yes, a Cattleya. It's very rare to see flowers of that colour. Especially in the tropics."

"I certainly wish we'd thought of spending our holiday in the airport before."

3

A blurred fluorescent light. Ian rubbed his eyes, wondering where he was. And then he remembered: one of the men's restrooms in the airport. He sat up carefully, so as not to wake Lydia, who was lying, dressed only in a white slip, beside him. But she was already stirring. He smiled fondly at her, thinking how fortunate he was to have such a sensitive, insightful wife. He felt absolutely certain that she alone of all women would be able to coax events of interest from every one of their days in the airport.

And yet over the last few weeks – months, really – he had been aware of a certain space between them. It was nothing he could really put into words, although he felt sure that Lydia herself felt exactly the same way. He wondered whether his old problem – sterility; they had never had children – could be at the root of it. Still, he told himself, it was hardly anything to worry about.

"Good morning, Ian," she whispered, opening her eyes.

"Good morning, my love. And it's all right. There's no need to whisper. I'm pretty sure we have the room to ourselves." He kissed her. "Did you sleep well?"

"Not at first, but it's supposed to be very therapeutic to sleep on a hard, flat surface. No doubt I'll feel quite rested in due course." She fumbled for her watch. "What's the time?"

"Seven. I'll have a shower in a minute, I think. Would you like me to see if there's anyone around so that you can slip out to the ladies'?"

She smiled wryly and stood. "It sounds so stagy, doesn't it? Just like our holiday in Greece, when we ran out of loose change and had to try to leave the hotel without porters demanding tips from us."

"Yes, I jumped every time I saw a uniform." He stood and took down his overnight bag from the space above the restroom bowl. Edging to one side so that there was room for Lydia, he took off his pyjamas, folded them, and then put on his dressing-gown. "What do you think we should do today?"

Lydia pushed her white-streaked hair away from her face and smiled mysteriously. "Well, no holiday is complete without looking up relatives!"

"Of course!" Ian pretended to slap his brow. "I forgot that your cousin Queenie works in customs. We haven't seen her in months!"

4

"Queenie! Long time no see!"

"Lydia?" A woman of about forty-five, blonde hair tucked into the cap of a uniform, looked up in surprise. "What are you doing here? Are you on holiday?"

"So to speak." Lydia's eyes twinkled.

"You look fantastic. You too, Ian Incroft!"

"I'm getting rather too many white hairs, I'm afraid," Lydia stated. "I must admit I'm thinking of getting it dyed my natural red."

"I wouldn't if I were you." Queenie checked her watch. "Look, I'll be going to morning tea in about ten minutes. Do you want to come with me?" Without waiting for a reply, she continued, slightly ruefully, "It really is fantastic to see you... but I suppose you're only here so you can jump on a plane?"

Ian smiled, and straightened the seam of his cream safari suit. "I can truthfully say that that is not the case."

"So do you fancy a mug of coffee?"

"Of course we do. Ten minutes will give us time to take a few snaps."

"Photographs? Of the airport?" Queenie narrowed her eyes, slightly confounded.

"I mean, Ian needs time to buy some film for his camera. It's quite reasonable here." She waved in the direction of a photo shop. "So we'll see you back here in about ten minutes."

As they approached the shop, Lydia stated jovially, "Well, why not take snaps of the airport? It's just as nice as any hotel. People don't realise that... *newness* can be found anywhere. People are too bound up with duty."

Ian squeezed her hand. "You're a genius, Lydia. The voice of reason."

5

"The door of this maintenance closet is worth a snap or two." Lydia was grasping the steel bar of a chair, critically contemplating the white wall in front of it.

Ian was unsure. "It certainly looks new, and it's freshly painted – but do you really think it's something we'd want to look at again?"

Lydia faced him, the acute angle of her nose seeming to divide the far wall of the airport. Then she closed her eyes, displaying the ginger lashes he always found so attractive. "Just consider it, Ian. How many people in the world have been into this closet? One? Two? Why, more people have been on Mount Everest than that! If we photograph this closet we'll have something that no one else has and we won't have risked our necks getting it."

Ian made a bemused nod. "You're right, of course. Accessibility isn't just a question of physical location. It's a question of attitude as well. You should have been a philosopher, Lyd. There's an opening at the Institute if you're interested in applying!"

She patted his hand. "So what angle shall we take?"

"Forty-five degrees I think. That way the dark seam between the door and the wall is most visible, and suggestive of the mysteries within." He manoeuvred himself into position, sighted the camera, and pressed the button. "We're real individuals, you and I."

Lydia paused, and then stated, matter-of-factly, "Then let's be even more individual and enter the closet!'

"Oh!" Ian was surprised. "Do you think we could?"

"Why not? I'll lock the door after us."

"Someone might see."

"So what if they do? I'm not aware of any 'No Admittance' sign."

Ian shrugged and drew open the door. He ushered Lydia inside and then closed it behind him.

The room contained a surprisingly large number of objects. In one corner was a floor polisher; it was the yellow of a tropical orchid. Cans of Tru-Sol were stacked on a high shelf. A row of white fluorescent lights shone pearl-like over a stack of coiled grey extension cords.

Lydia nudged one of the extension cords with the toe of her high heels. "This reminds me of that adder we saw at the snake farm in Malaysia. Remember?"

"How could I forget? I hate snakes."

"So do I." She sighed. "It makes you wonder why we spent money looking over a snake farm, doesn't it."

"So much of what human beings do is unconscious. It's all dreamlike, smoky. I see it every day, teaching at the institute. You tell students, especially the non-religious ones, to paint an abstract work and they nearly always fall back on realism." He brushed some motes from his safari suit. "Next time I want them to paint a snake maybe I should ask them to paint this extension cord instead."

Lydia's eyes widened. "Ian, you're brilliant."

"I know." He kissed her. "But in what particular way am I being brilliant now?"

"What you just said. We needn't confine ourselves even to the airport! This room has everything you'd expect from a holiday – in abstract form!"

6

Lydia had rearranged the cans of Tru-Sol in a geometric pattern beside her handbag, which she had placed next to the floor-polisher. "This will be to the traditional holiday what an abstract work of art is to the realist."

"So we photograph the extension cord, and let it stand for the snakes we saw in Malaysia?"

"Exactly."

"What about food?"

"We still have those blue fruits, don't forget."

"Blue fruits, with gold pulp," Ian reflected. "The sky and the sun, for our consumption alone." He drew himself up. "And what about the looking-up-relatives aspect of a holiday?"

"We'll simply leaf through my address book. When you think about it, everything about people is conjured up by their names anyway." She gingerly lowered herself on to the white tiles, motioned to Ian to sit beside her. "Let's start with the names beginning with A."

"The Ayres," Ian said, reading over her shoulder. "Remember them?"

"How could I not? She lacked breeding, and those cigars of his made me want to strangle him."

"It was her watery eyes that used to nettle me. If contact lenses disagreed with her so much, why did she wear them?"

"People don't think."

Ian took her hand. Its lines reminded him of the contours of some map. "Who's on page B?"

"The Beauchamps. Now I think we should see more of them. Although the way they kept trying to trump our holidays was tedium itself."

"They won't be able to trump this one."

"True." She closed her eyes. "You know, Ian... there's no real need to read this address book either. We know who's in it. We can picture them in front of our eyes."

"The true life is the life of the mind," Ian intoned.

"Exactly," Lydia replied.

"So you're suggesting?"

7

Ian wondered how long he had been sitting with his eyes closed. Time and space, he remembered the philosopher Kant had written, were shared by the inner and the outer worlds, so the question was not a meaningless one. But he had promised Lydia that he would not check his watch, or, indeed, try to interact with the outer world at all.

Still, it was cooler now. That meant that somewhere 'outside' of him – almost as though in another part of the world – Lydia was now at a greater distance. She always had been, he realised suddenly – and felt an immense relief knowing that he had at last put his finger on what had recently been worrying him.

But there was nothing they could do about such separation. Ultimately, it was an irreducible abstraction, a metaphor – just as it was now abstract and metaphorical to refer to countries they had visited; airports they had inhabited; and closets they had entered.

Significant Other

1

Matt sat in the lounge and stared at Elsie's empty chair. It had been empty for four months and every day he wondered with an increasing frustration whether it would always be empty. The shadow-grey felt of the chair and its design of faded abstract flowers did little to lift his spirits.

He still couldn't believe that someone who, for twenty-four years, had felt a part of him could suddenly just leave. True, he had often teased her for a laugh but it was not as though he had committed adultery or even broken any promises. She had simply informed him that she could not resign herself to their everyday routine, the boredom of life with him since his early retirement. Perhaps she was going through a mid-life crisis. She was forty-four. But all the medical literature he had read denied the reality of 'midlife crisis' as a valid scientific concept. He told himself he'd blame God, if he felt able to believe in something he couldn't perceive.

Clearly today was going to be one of his 'bad days'. Suddenly angry to the point of tears he grasped a long strand of his greying, though still voluminous and mane-like hair and used it to wipe the corner of his eyes. His stubby index finger (he had lost the tip of it in a mine-site accident years ago) brushed his nose. Immediately he thought of Elsie's nose, her most distinctive feature. It was certainly not an attractive nose – it was, indeed, rather long and florid – but these aspects marked it out as uniquely hers. In fact, he realised, he could picture every detail of Elsie in his mind, almost as though she were standing in front of him.

He closed his eyes, longing to picture more. The blue dress with the polka dots that many considered frumpish but which he thought really suited her – he could almost trace mentally its folds and cut. And her pink casuals, the ones with spacings between the straps like the gills of a fish – their ellipses could not be sharper if he were actually looking at them.

Perhaps, he mused with a heavy whimsicality, Elsie really hadn't left him after all. Perhaps she was simply in the other room. That would explain how he could envisage her so clearly. If she had really left four months ago, she'd surely be just a fading memory by now.

He stared at the door leading to the kitchen, aware that many times he had sat in this very position, with Elsie quietly intent on some task not apparent to him. He had been relatively happy on those times, he reflected, and he was in a similar situation now. So why shouldn't he be happy again?

Yes, he told himself: he would pretend – if 'pretend' was really the right word – that Elsie was still with him. The world would be as he wanted it to be for a change!

"Elsie," he called. "You know the wallpaper you suggested? Was it vermilion with a red motif that you wanted, or red with a vermilion motif?"

There was no reply. No doubt, he forced himself to believe, she went on to the porch while he was drifting away in his armchair. How just like Elsie, the silly scatterbrain, always zigzagging off on some errand! Or drinking too much hock and saying, "Ooh wow!" before falling asleep in her chair, her eyelids like the folds on the canopy of a four-poster bed...

2

As he stepped into the bright sunshine, the clothes hoist like a spider web against the umber, lichen-dotted roofs, he saw that his neighbour on the right, Mark Styles, was leaning over the fence, his head almost lost among the sunflowers.

"Haven't seen Elsie about for a while, Matt. She all right?"

Matt thought quickly. Then, "No, actually. She has this mole on her left temple. She's going to see a specialist, but until the appointment it's obviously best for her to keep out of the sun."

"Yes, that's sensible. For a while I thought you might have given the old cheese the push for the insurance. All that leisure time to play with!"

Matt made no effort to prevent an icy tone from entering his voice. "Elsie is the most precious part of my life. Saying that is beyond the pale." He stared at Styles as though he were an imbecile.

"Sorry, Matt."

"That's all right. We can't all have consideration. Anyway, I expect she's cooking up something fantastic this very moment so I'll be going inside." Without waiting for a reply, he gestured to Styles, and went back into the passage.

The kitchen table was bare, of course. Again he thought quickly. Was it possible that Elsie had said, at some time, something to the effect that *he* would have to do the cooking today? It certainly wasn't impossible that she had. It certainly didn't break any laws of physics. He found himself thinking of his old days at the university, learning for his physics degree the principles of mechanical engineering, stress and torque – and, as electives, a unit or two of astronomy and philosophy. He couldn't remember much about the philosophy units, except that they had emphasized everything was 'textual', and that they had contained a great many catch-phrases and expressions, like 'sun of truth', *'différance'*, and 're-mark'. But yes, he told himself, Elsie could easily be lying down in the spare bedroom, leaving the cooking to him. He'd be quiet in case he roused her. Nevertheless, he couldn't stop himself from whistling softly, almost happily, the main theme from the *Local Hero* soundtrack.

As he briskly took a lettuce and two eggs from the refrigerator, and then set about finding the Worcestershire sauce, olive oil and parmesan cheese, he remembered that Elsie wasn't fond of Caesar salad. So there would be no point in taking a bowl of it into the spare bedroom.

3

"Mr Rendall? My name is Olivia Nugent. I'm a social worker. Helpline passed on your details to me when you rang last week, so I'm calling on you to see if there's anything I can do."

It was nine o'clock the next day and Matt rubbed his eyes, having only just woken from his first sound sleep in four months. He tried to focus on the social worker. Not only were his eyes filmy but he was also becoming long-sighted. After a few seconds he made out a slim, gawky woman with a roll of nut-brown hair that looked as though it were intended to be eased into an air-hostess's cap. She was also wearing an absurdly voluminous, loose-woven jumper, and matching dun slacks.

"That's nice of you. Even first thing in the morning," Matt retorted. "I suppose you'd better follow me. You'll have to put up with the house being a bit of a sty at the moment."

"Thank you." She strode past him into the passage and then turned. "The details I was given implied you were practically beside yourself after your wife left. 'Nettie', wasn't it?"

"Elsie." Matt stared in amused disbelief at her pushiness, and then adopted a smug smile. "I'm happy to say that's all changed!"

"You mean she's come back? I'm so relieved for you!" Olivia Nugent clasped her hands together, and then looked about. "Would you still like me to have a talk with her? Something low-key? Sometimes a third party can put to rest any lingering little issues, and despite a rapprochement, there *are* always lingering issues."

"She's lying in the spare bedroom right now. She has a mole on her temple and doesn't want to talk about it. I don't want her roused."

"Of course. I'm with you." Olivia Nugent reached for his hand, which she shook. "Mr Rendall, I'll leave my details with you, you never know... but let me say how relieved I am that everything has been resolved so fantastically."

Matt shrugged. "Thanks. So am I. That goes without saying. When you think about it, the human condition is such that there's always some separation between people, isn't there?

Presence and absence. It's just a question of deciding the degree of absence you can live with."

The social worker clearly didn't follow his meaning but she quickly disguised her expression so that there was just bubbly warmth. (Matt found himself thinking of champagne that had been left out in the sun.) "Exactly. You have a nice day, Mr Rendall."

<h1 style="text-align:center">4</h1>

As the months passed, Matt realised that his relationship with Elsie had never been better. She was the ideal wife, he told himself, never imposing her presence on him, never noisy, always giving him space, yet simultaneously always *there*, just out of sight. He wondered how he ever could have thought she'd left him. It was not the sort of thing she'd do. She was too considerate, too deferential. A far more likely explanation for his recent worries was that he had been having mental delusions. So far as Elsie was concerned, clearly all that had happened lately was that she had grown even more deferential than usual.

He thought over the past weeks. For her birthday he had bought her a Wedgewood cake slice he'd always admired and, as it was purely for decoration, he'd arranged it next to her jewel box. How like her, he reflected, not to have moved it, thus implicitly complimenting him on his discernment in arranging decorations! He began to make vague plans for her Christmas present. Elsie tended to sequester herself in the kitchen most of Christmas day, of course, wrestling with the plum duff and the forcemeat (she always grew flustered when he made suggestions while she was trying to cook); but a little surprise, perhaps hidden somewhere so that they could later play the 'Treasure Hunt' game that had always given him pleasure in the early days of their relationship, would be enthusiastically received. It wouldn't matter if she took a while to find the present. They had plenty of time.

And space, he thought contentedly, lying back in his armchair with his eyes closed. Empty space, true, but finite space, space that had to end somewhere with the presence of Elsie. That was a fact, because the infinite was physically meaningless, even if some maintained space was made up of an infinite number of mathematical points. Elsie would always be only a finite distance from him, until – ghastly thought! – she died.

There was a scrabbling at the door, followed by a bang. Startled, Matt sat up, checked the time. It was eight in the evening. What could be responsible? He started down the passage, apprehensive. He was short and even in his younger days he had been physically weak (although he was sure he would have been a success at karate). Clearly, he decided, if there were about to be a home invasion there would be little he could do to defend himself. Nevertheless he wondered whether there was time to retrieve the poker from the lounge.

But the door was already open.

"It's me Matt. I'm back." There was an exhausted groan. "Ooh wow, this case is heavy. I'm so sorry about the last weeks. I don't know what possessed me. But I'm back on track. It's important to know the good guys and the bad guys, isn't it?"

For a few moments Matt simply stood there. Then he turned away, smiling at his imagination. Ahead of him he could see the dining room and its rows of champagne flutes, like tears that had been frozen and thus would never, ever fall. "As far as I'm concerned, Elsie, nothing has changed," he stated to the air, looking at her empty chair and thinking of the curvature of the earth and possibly of space itself.

Tim's Howse

1

Jim regards his jigsaw puzzle. Its far edge looks shiny: the fire is reflected in it. The flames shift, as though the winter wind is inhaling them up the flue. He feels cosy.

The jigsaw is of a child building a kennel. It has the words 'Tim's Howse'. He wonders if only the word 'howse' is misspelled. Perhaps 'Tim' is a misspelling of 'time'. But he has never been much with spelling. He isn't very bright; he's just a storeman. On the other hand, he's lucky to have a job.

He scrabbles among them, the pieces, for one with a bright vermilion line. The puzzle has a lot of pieces like that.

He doesn't find the piece, but finds part of the dog. He feels cheered. He always likes to finish the dog before anything else. But is it normal to be so involved with jigsaws? He hasn't had any romance for a while, but is that his fault? Perhaps God is punishing him for some reason. Still, if he had someone they'd only spend his money. And there's plenty of time. He is still in his twenties. He could meet someone at the stores one day. He might even find someone willing to put up with his grinding teeth at night.

He lifts his glass of whisky. Its shade is like that of parts of the jigsaw. He inhales the thick scent. Alcohol isn't really a drug. He is against drugs, like his father. If he ever found himself involved with a drug-taker it would be the finish. At least jigsaws don't harm anyone.

He taps the cardboard surface of the table-leg. He can feel the seam where two pieces are butting. Hard together. How far across the room does the jigsaw reach tonight? He is halfway through, so probably the same. The puzzle can sometimes even reach the ceiling, although not many people know that. Once, old Donna from the canteen had dropped around but she hadn't even noticed the pieces. She never notices anything, except how many eggs her ducks are laying. But he doesn't really blame her. Apparently her first husband often beat her. He'd feel sorry for anyone who had to put up with that. Still, it would have been nice to prise the pieces from the wall and show her what was beneath them.

At this thought, he stirs. Even he doesn't know what is beneath the pieces. He has always wanted to look, but there have always been more pressing things. Like the new lampshade he'd had to put up.

Suddenly, he wonders if he's too timid to look beneath the pieces. He's never had much pluck. He doesn't even know how to drive. But at least when he was in that car with the shattered windscreen he'd been the one to keep cool. He'd merely said, half in fun, "Woe is me."

He stands. He will look now. At worst, probably, his slacks could get dirty – although he'll watch out, naturally.

After some thought, he settles on a section of the wall near a small spider's web. That way, he'll have a guide to replace the pieces. He climbs on a chair and examines the web. Then he gingerly removes a piece at eye-level, feeling awkwardly daft at the idea of someone coming in now. Trizzy Liz would make out he'd seen a mouse. He removes another piece.

Soon, he has created an egg-shaped section but so far he can see nothing. He stands on tip-toe, hoping he isn't damaging the finish on his casuals; then leans forward, teetering.

There's another room!

He draws away more pieces. Now he can see them, boards. They are the shade of the buff stationery he is always ordering. But why does the room seem familiar?

Of course! It's like Tim's Howse! He ducks so that he can edge through the hole. He feels even more enthusiastic than he did on the guided tour of the facsimile Elizabethan cottage. He wonders why he has always been fascinated by the past.

"What can I do for you?"

Starting, he turns – and sees an old woman. Her hair is mouse-coloured.

He feels silly. "I didn't know anyone... was here. I'll go back."

"No, come in. I get very bored on my own. Would you like some tea? You can call me Mrs J."

He pauses reluctantly. He isn't very hungry. He bought a pie and chips and two large chicken rolls at Chris's, just after work.

"Well then?"

All at once, he is decided. "You have a way with words." Telling himself that he's incorrigible, he lowers himself into the room. He hopes the woman can't see the hole in her wall. She looks short-sighted, so perhaps she thinks it's just a door. He'd better not mention jigsaws.

"A way with words?" She beams. "Yes, that's certainly right. One of my pastimes is to take all sorts of common objects and see how many different surprising things I can write about them."

He smiles. He can't think of a reply.

"Would you like me to show you?"

"All right."

"Well, what objects? Have you anything on you, or can you think of something?" She taps her fingers.

He concentrates. All he can think of is disco music, for some reason, but she probably wouldn't know what that was. In fact, it's a while since he went to a disco. He can never hear anything and they always charge too much. He reaches into his jumper and takes out some cents. "Is this what you mean?"

She purses her lips. "That is quite suitable. Now, what can I say?" She examines the coins. "Of course. Native animals. Have you ever wondered why Australian coins have animals, while Australian notes have famous people? The implication is that the difference between animals and, say, that writer on the five dollar bill is just a few cents." She cackles.

He doesn't follow it, her drift... He looks around for a door. It might be better to leave through one, rather than the hole.

"What do you think?"

He shrugs.

"Well? I'm no Job, you know."

Again he shrugs.

She leans close to him. "You're a very stolid young man. You don't seem to have any drive."

He is taken aback; he puts his hands on his hips. "Oh! Well, let's put it this way. I didn't ask to come in. You made me."

"Be my guest, then, and leave!" She turns away.

Without a word, he starts towards the hole. He does have drive. He often has a flutter on the horses, for example.

2

The following evening, he lights the fire and then goes to the turntable. He is still embarrassed after yesterday but he's determined to block out the whole affair. He selects a Jim Nabors record, depresses the needle and then returns to his chair.

He contemplates Tim's Howse. He seems to have lost his enthusiasm for it. He absently takes a large bite from his hot dog. It is part of the special offer he saw on the ad during *Sale of the Century*. He shakes his head, tries to concentrate. Maybe that woman will complain about him, or his jigsaws. He regards the section of the wall with the spider's web – and sits up.

He can't see the pieces!

Quickly, he approaches the wall.

They're barely apparent, the seams... He tries to decide what to do. Obviously that woman has altered the nature of the room. He draws over the chair but then recalls his father's 'saw': 'with any relationship if there are problems the first time there'll be problems the second'. It would be better just to think about the jigsaw and the fire and the peaceful sounds of Jim Nabors and hope that everything will be normal.

He begins to search for a piece, but then stops. He can't concentrate, knowing that the room has altered.

He will have to visit her, after all. Maybe she'll cooperate. She may be just a lonely old woman.

Climbing on to the chair, he taps a seam, and then prises some pieces off. Chips of plaster, like flour or ground bone.

Soon he is through the wall. He gingerly dusts his slacks.

"Back again, I see."

Before him is the woman. She is taking a book from a solid-looking desk. Close are a gas-ring and a tea-cosy.

He tries to collect his thoughts. "That's right." He puts his hands on his hips, and draws in some air. "What are your intentions with my room?"

"I don't know what you mean, I'm sure."

"You must." He fixes her with an expression of wounded accusation. "You said you like surprising things."

"Yes." She sighs. "But I'd rather not go into hows and whys, now. My veins today… I have this complaint…"

He tries not to show his sympathy. "But my room has altered."

"You have, I'd say. Your manner, at least."

He peers at her. From this position, her expression is like that of a girl he'd taken a shine to, at a disco a few years back. He'd winked at her but she'd made out that she hadn't seen. "I don't follow."

"Well, the impression I had of you yesterday was that you don't like change. Now, you seem more open."

He feels put out but uncertain. He starts towards the hole, then turns. He'll show her that he's still in charge! "I haven't changed. There's obviously no point in being here, so I'm going."

She raises a worn hand.

As he climbs back, he finds himself musing on her age. She could be a hundred, easily. But that's not important. Now that he's asserted himself, he can continue with Tim's Howse.

3

He looks up from his jigsaw. It's late. The fire is spent. What time is it? The puzzle is finished, except for the dog. He seems to have mislaid the pieces. He places his fingers in the gap and watches the seam draw on to all five of them, the lines starting to crisscross his hand.

Myths of the K Mart

1

It is winter. Mark peers at his watch. Eight twenty-five. In five minutes he will be allowed in the K Mart. When he leaves the store, around five thirty, the light will be as faint as it is now. He smiles to think that entry to the K Mart is dependent on the position of the sun. But at least staff are allowed in the store both earlier and later than customers; he feels slightly superior.

The K Mart where he is a casual is unique in that some days it becomes one of the ball-and-maze games which are sold at the toy counter. They are the only days he enjoys. He loves pressing his back against the plastic wall, hearing a sinister rumbling; then watching Mrs Salom's face pale as the metal ball careers towards her.

Today, unfortunately, is probably not one in which the K Mart will be the maze-game. Resigned, he again checks the time, sees it is eight thirty, enters the parting glass doors, and approaches the counter.

He is here before Mrs Salom, his superior, of course. He stares up at the corrugated passage that is the air-conditioning duct. It reminds him of a stiff earthworm. Once, someone had said his manner was 'stiff' but that was just because he reads a lot.

Mrs Salom is drawing near. He loves taking the rise out of her. A lean woman with a wrinkled neck, she has iron-ore coloured hair, which is always in a top-knot. The sleek, shiny hairs are like those on a Christmas tree decoration.

She regards him resolutely. "Morning, Mark. Standing by doing nothing I see." She points. "That display needs seeing too. Rise and shine!"

Piqued, he tries to sound urbane. "All right. I'm not pressed for time right now."

"You can start by taking that mannequin back to the red light stand. How it got here I can't think." She indicates a mannequin in the aisle. Its base is against a Vulcan heater.

He stirs. He likes handling mannequins – even goosing them. Why is his sex drive so strong? He's never been able to talk openly to girls. They always seem to be involved with religious groups. He's been out with only one: Kaylene. But that was a crush, not love. From the corner of his eye, he sees Mrs Salom is not looking. He snakes out his left hand and grasps the mannequin's calf. Immediately, he feels guilt. Is he normal? Clearly it would be abnormal to have sex with a dummy, but nothing else, surely. He shakes his head. Sometimes he can't understand himself.

He seizes the mannequin, shoves it forward. It grazes the heater and becomes stuck. He inhales deeply, weary at the thought of having to exert himself. If only he had some other job! Perhaps he could work in the bar over the road. No, his father has told him that alcohol is a drug of dependence. But that was just because he was a miner. All miners are 'in their cups', as his mother says.

Suddenly, he pauses. He can hear a dull sound, like that in a bowling alley before a strike.

He was wrong! The K Mart will be the maze-game today!

Entranced, he stares into the corners of the building, waiting for the walls to become the familiar colour of asparagus soup or pus.

One by one the counters become plastic. Racks of clothing fuse into one another, forming clear passages. Mrs Salom turns and sighs. She knows what will happen next. He begins to crow as she darts into the aisle, glancing to her left, her right, trying to spot the ball. She ducks as the layer of colourless plastic forms over the passage.

And then he sees the ball. As always, it is massive and awe-inspiring, thundering down the passage that led to men's wear. Mrs Salom staggers but nips into a side-passage just in time. He runs after the ball, hooting with delight.

76

2

"What are you trying to do to me? You'll have me in an early grave!"

Mark starts. Surely the old pain isn't blaming him for the maze-game? No, that was yesterday morning. There has always been a mutual understanding that there will be no allusions to their shared activity. What, then, is she going on about?

She points to the wool display, where old ladies are running worn claws over sky-coloured yarn. "I told you yesterday to sort out the colours! How can a customer find the colour they're after if they're all mixed up?"

"The shop lifters don't seem to have problems." Often he has seen grannies coolly pocket lumps of wool. His usual response is to smile accommodatingly at them, cheered that the old souls are able to beat the system. He would never attract the attention of Esteban, the store detective. There would only be a scene. Besides, Esteban is thick. Once, he had asked him whether he wanted a cup of tea, and he had replied, "Que?"

"...the whole point of your life, to needle me? How dare you address me like that!"

"Oh, get knotted." He stalks away. He doubts that even the maze-game could save him today. Why is he always lumped in with idiots? Are they necessary, so that those who aren't become more noticeable? He contemplates the stationery counter. Nearby, women are passing over last summer's gilt-framed sunglasses. Some of the panes, he notes absently, are perfectly circular.

Hands seize him. He is whirled around and sees a tomato topped with steel wool: an incensed Mrs Salom.

The walls become green. There is a sound like thunder. The hands release him.

He is astounded. He had thought the maze-game's appearance even less likely today than yesterday but Mrs Salom is haring for the book section so it must be coming. He watches, entranced yet disconcerted, as she peers from behind a stand of *Reader's Digests*.

The ball rumbles round a corner, bearing down on her: then, it swoops upwards! Soon it is above the ground floor, soaring higher into the matrix of three dimensional passages which has suddenly surrounded him like some crystal hive.

What has caused the change to three dimensions? Absorbed, he wanders among the passages, staring up through the thick colourless plastic. How many storeys are there? Thirty? Perhaps an infinite number! Mrs Salom is now on the fifth one, but the ball has shot straight to the eighth. Clearly it will land near the well just in front of her.

He smiles darkly. She will have difficulty eluding the ball now.

3

The following morning he feels out of sorts. He can think only of the change to the maze-game. For the first time, he wonders whether it is real, or has any meaning. But of course it doesn't. He knows from the lyrics of new wave groups that life is meaningless. He becomes aware of the beat from the stereo section.

Mrs Salom says something but he can't follow what. Several times already today she has ticked him off, and he has hardly noticed. Perhaps the maze-game will appear soon.

Perhaps the ball will kill her.

And then around him is the three-dimensional matrix. He is startled. Maybe he merely has to will the game into existence! But where is Mrs Salom? He looks about and sees her on the fourth layer, right in one corner. The ball is on the second, zig-zagging up.

He approaches a well and begins to climb. It is a trial; he has to pause to catch his breath. Then he looks down and sees that he is above what was the lay-by counter. The passages are like the creeks of some geometric map. Is the maze-game, then, a map of the K Mart? No, he tells himself; the maze-game is more important than the K Mart. In the real world, the K Mart is probably just the set of instructions that enables the toy-counter maze-game to be solved. Or maybe both ideas are true! Maybe, in the real world, you are supposed to use the maze-game as a map or atlas to explore the K Mart, so that you are sufficiently familiar with the K Mart to solve the maze-game. Like a legend. He touches his finger-tips, and then recalls Mrs Salom.

Fortunately she has descended to the third layer so there will be fewer tiers to climb. The ball is on the fifth floor. Perhaps it will drive her down to his level. He edges forward so that he is directly beneath her. Guiltily and slightly revolted he stares up her dress. He sees folds of cloth, like the lace around a mushroom stalk. He closes his eyes.

Suddenly, he hears a cry and Mrs Salom is hurtling down a shaft. She strikes the ground floor and is still. The ball slows as it reaches the shaft. Then it shakes slightly and begins to roll backwards.

He is disturbed. The ball is after him! But why? Soon it will be close enough to touch.

He throws himself on to the next layer, looking behind. He wonders suddenly whether he will have to spend whole days darting among the clear passages. If only he had been a store detective! But he'd have needed his Leaving for that. And there'd be too many rules – like the K Mart itself: invisible borders, nets formed by aisles and tills.

He begins to run. His mind feels increasingly in pieces, shot through by light from memories of the steamy window of the rotisserie, seas of fleecy waistcoats pouring through the doors. He can see them already in the carpark, flying into the air across Richmond Road, across entire states; is that what is meant by inflation projections?

And then the ball crashes through the plastic on his right.

Back to the Bars

1

As Wayne turned down Townsend Road, he was surprised to find that he recognised none of its houses. But that, he quickly told himself, was because the last time he visited the street (over ten years ago) he had been devoting all his attention to the car he was trying to follow.

He noted the numbers on the letter-boxes. Ten... eight. He had arrived. He felt even more surprised. Was the house before him really the one where the red-headed woman had lived? It appeared not only unfamiliar but also strangely repellent. The walls were a shade of buff he found unprepossessing and the verandah-posts had the moulded, chess piece kind of appearance that he had always thought pointless.

True, his last visit had been at one in the morning, when little was in sharp relief – but the woman had actually drawn his attention towards certain aspects of the house. The extensions that had just been completed; the massive chandelier with multi-faceted panes and panels suspended from gold bars of different lengths; even the musical box that had played a Mozart rondo: he could almost see these objects before him. The woman had told him she loved antiques – she had worked for a removal firm that specialised in them – but Wayne wished that he had asked her more about herself. He wasn't even sure of her name. Over ten years ago she'd told him to give her a ring but he hadn't wanted to get involved. He knew that if he weren't so self-absorbed he'd feel ashamed of this inaction. Really, he was a criminal who ought to crave punishment. Still, there was nothing he could do to rectify matters now.

From the corner of his eye, he saw that across the road a man, who was bald except for two lumps of curly grey hair like ear-muffs, was watching him suspiciously. Reluctantly, he glanced at the house once more and then started back along the road. If only it were still one in the morning, March 1997! He'd always loved autumn and autumn 1997 had a special quality. But how could he go back in time?

Reaching his car, he opened the door and sat. He stared at the dashboard. The graduations on the meter were like a drawing of a rising or a setting sun. He recalled that this image had always suggested itself to him. It was hackneyed, he mused, but some things never changed.

So why shouldn't he pretend it was March 1997, still?

For several moments, he merely sat, absorbed by the idea. What, after all, had really changed between 1997 and the present? In a certain sense, the past never went away. The whole of civilisation depended on this idea. On a more personal level, he could still pass for someone in his twenties and there were only minor differences between his present lifestyle and that of 1997.

Deciding to make a list of everything he could recall about March 1997, he opened the glove box and withdrew his antique fountain pen (it was an heirloom) and a pad. Then he contemplated the steering wheel. The most important difference between now and 1997, he realised, was that in 1997 the Liberal Party had been in power in this state. Still, it was a cliché that life under the two parties differed only marginally. He jotted down 'Liberal Party'. The paper gave a little as he supported it with his hand. Next, he told himself, books: what had he been reading in 1997? Philosophy, of course, but also *Axel*. He had always enjoyed reading about castles. He was virtually a prisoner to good writing. Classical music reminded him of castles so he'd also have to listen to that. He invariably did, anyway. The sound of the oboe inevitably seemed to capture the feeling of autumn.

He stared at the rows of houses on his right. He'd still been boarding with his aunt in 1997 so he'd have to move back with her. She'd be delighted. It would no doubt recall to her memories of his early childhood when she would hint at misdemeanours he might commit and then take pleasure in punishing him when he did so (perhaps only half-suspecting he was half-enjoying the punishments as well). He tapped the gold medallion she had bought him and then admired himself in the mirror. The medallion seemed surrounded by faint ghost rings. He moved so that his expression appeared slightly wistful. From some angles, he looked 'dashing', as they used to say. Certainly women had always flocked around him. His hair was the colour of a freshly-minted dollar coin; and it swept away from his elliptical face and high cheekbones as though it wished to emphasise the separateness of body and spirit.

All at once, he was resolved. Tonight he would go to Matches, the bar he had frequented in 1997. He had stopped going there when they suddenly doubled their ten dollar cover charge but he told himself that if he were to pass the doorman one ten dollar note on top of another he could enter and also pretend that he was behaving as he had in 1997.

He examined the list. Then he closed his eyes.

2

As he pulled into the parking lot, he checked his watch. He'd be first in the bar, as always. He withdrew from his deck his cassette of oboe concertos. It clicked like a mousetrap.

Outside Matches, he contemplated the door. Of embossed, imitation copper, with a high lustre, its great size gave the impression it wouldn't look out of place on a castle. He drew it open, paid the doorman (who nodded silently and vaguely) and began to ascend the stairs.

He was in a darkness, a darkness that flashed, and pulsed, in time to a racket; a mirrored ball, like some stylised naval mine, whirled dizzyingly.

As soon as his eyes adjusted to the lighting, he stared around the room. Packed. He had never known it to be so crowded. He must have made a mistake with the time. Confounded, he barged through it, the sea of people, so that she – whoever he struck up a conversation with – wouldn't know that he'd just come in. He didn't want to appear too eager, after all.

He saw a woman sitting by herself. Peering at her, he felt an increasing attraction. The ambiguous lighting conditions meant the colour of her hair was hard to discern but it was in the shape of two mathematical integration-signs placed back to back. Her nose was aquiline, her eyes as undecidable as her hair. He moved closer.

The woman looked up and regarded him with an expression of barely-checked enthusiasm. "Hi, young guy," she projected her words above the racket, "Crowded, isn't it?"

Wayne leaned close to make himself heard. "Right! And I thought I'd have the place to myself."

"Did you have far to come?"

"No. What about you?"

"Just a short way. You know St Anne's by the river?"

"Not Townsend Road!"

"How did you know?"

He paused, unaccountably apprehensive. "What number?"

"Eight."

He felt himself sit beside her. Was she playing a joke on him? He felt sure she was nothing like the woman at number eight, although it was true he couldn't remember her well. Could one of his old flames have put her up to it? They must have done – it couldn't be a coincidence!

And yet no one knew that he had intended to visit Matches tonight.

He shook his head. Every day, he realised, people won sweepstakes. Surely the fact that this person lived at eight Townsend Road was no more far-fetched than that. Certainly the possibility – which he felt silly even to consider – that he had actually gone back in time was far less likely. Time travel, he knew, was regarded by physicists as almost a crime against the laws of nature. Yet wasn't memory a form of time travel? And Leibniz had said something about 'the identity of indiscernibles'.

He decided to play it cool. "Nice place, is it?"

The woman glanced drily at him. "We can go and see, if you like."

"Fantastic." In spite of his disconcertment – on a different level it occurred to him that he should also be surprised by her attitude – he felt himself grow deliciously tense. "Have you got a car? If you have I can follow."

"No problem."

He stood; the woman did so as well.

3

She was a reckless driver! He could barely keep up – with the tail-lights of her maroon (or was it black?) Sonata – as they dashed from lane to lane. Fortunately, they'd just passed the flyover so they'd be at Townsend Road soon, despite all the antics. He found himself kneading the wheel. He could still barely credit the coincidence of it all.

And then her car pulled in. They had arrived.

He stepped from his car and drew his blazer around himself. The air was brisk. But he loved being out late. He always had. He felt a certain frisson in knowing not only that while ninety per cent of the population was asleep he was fully conscious and therefore in control but also that he was a potential victim of the night and anything it might conceal.

"I'll see about some coffee." Opening the door, the woman gestured inside.

Wayne nodded and stepped over the mat. It had an image of a portcullis. When his eyes adjusted to the darkness, he saw a passage: it had Queen Anne tables (the legs of which made him think of parentheses), a huge chandelier, a bureau with a musical box. But after what had happened in Matches, he was barely surprised that the passage corresponded with the one he remembered.

The woman steered him into the kitchen. Then she filled the jug and simultaneously turned on an antique wooden record player. He moved forwards to examine it. No, he saw: the wooden 'record player' was just a box. It actually housed compact and modern audio equipment. As the power came on there was a faint rumble, followed by the grating of synthesisers.

"I love this track. I hope you don't mind. It's the latest by Jaussa-Jaussa-Jaussa." She began to reel about in time to the beat.

"Go ahead." He feigned an accommodating smile, and sat by the table. He'd been weighing up several avenues of small talk, but for some reason he could only think of politics. At least, he mused, the catchy, ghastly single or whatever it was, meant he needn't say anything. He contemplated the woman, suddenly disturbed. Why was he so wooden towards other people? Sometimes he didn't understand himself.

The single stopped. The woman turned off the jug. "Shall we have sex?"

Heart racing, Wayne nodded.

4

The following morning he woke after falling back, several times, in his usual morning daze. He sat up. His bedroom arced, as though he were in the arms of a dancing woman. Did he really have to get out of bed today?

He moved to check the time, caught the scent of smoke from his hair.

Beneath his watch was a piece of yellow notepaper! He picked it up. Handwriting. He must have exchanged his address with the woman before he went home after sex. Like a pact. Had he really been to Townsend Road? Absently, he massaged his temples. Whatever, she had him now. Any second the phone would ring, and he'd have to make a decision.

No! He would seize the moment and ring her. Shuffling into his slippers, he went to the phone, lifted the receiver, dialed.

"Ruth here."

He was faintly nonplussed. Was that right, Ruth? Quickly, he went, "Hi. It's Wayne."

"Oh, hi! How are you after last night? It's a pity you couldn't stay longer."

"Fantastic." He realised his face was beaming. "And you?"

"A bit under the weather, but the same apart from that. Say, do you want to come over this afternoon?"

He felt a prick of apprehension, as the centuries of a binding relationship flashed before him. "Tonight... would be better." He sought a pretext. "I'm giving my brother a hand with moving."

"What time then? Five? Four? We could go and get something to eat."

He felt himself melting. Silently, he sighed. "Two would be fine."

"Unreal. I'll see you then then. Bye."

"Bye." He replaced the receiver. He was imprisoned. He could almost see himself at the dock, or even the altar.

He closed his eyes. For all he knew, they could be together in ten years.

Another Fall Myth

1

As I make my way along the track, I find myself reflecting on the moment, twelve months ago, when I first caught sight of the Bridge. The moment had had a mystical quality. The autumn shadows had been shifting like dark mirrors, seeming to bear to the bleached bottles and broken window panes beneath the Bridge much more than the simple relationship of black to white.

I glance at the bush. The landscape does not provide any indications that the Bridge is close but that, I know, means nothing.

Soon, eucalypts surrounds me and grey-green bushes I cannot identify. Their leaves are sharp-edged like the cross-section of a staircase. I draw aside some branches and see a wooden object. For several moments I merely stand, wondering if I have succeeded. The object before me certainly looks like the Bridge, and below it there are plenty of shattered panes, but the atmosphere is not right. The scene does not have the feeling of autumn. Before, the setting had had the indefinable autumn character that I associate with such places as the Conservatory and the Night Club.

Could I be losing my sensitivity to autumn?

Reluctantly, I move back towards the car. I shall revisit the Conservatory, I decide, and find out that way.

2

It has always seemed to me that autumnal peace is threaded in the very air of the Conservatory. The trickling water and the knots of crotons, orchids and Moses-in-the-bulrushes always make me feel as I do when the nights start to grow longer and the wind starts to develop a certain edge.

I climb the concrete steps that lead to the second storey of the Conservatory. The view is better from above; there is a small platform that lets one take in most of the plants. Unfortunately, also visible from the platform is the river, and the river always reminds me of summer. But I reflect that if I start inadvertently to dwell on summer, I merely need to stare down at the crotons or recall some of my Autumn Moments. These moments include the evening I had spent listening to Liszt, and the one when I had tried to teach myself to play the oboe.

Reaching the platform, I feel relieved that I am alone. Whenever I am with someone else, I find it hard to concentrate on autumn. In fact, of all the popular places I know, only the Night Club reminds me of it. I must have spent hours in the Night Club, admiring its red oak panels and staring at the multiple reflections in the bar's mirror. Sometimes I have actually gone up to people because of a certain character in the autumn light.

How distant those times seem!

I make my way down the stairs, concerned. *Why* do the times seem distant? Clearly, I shall have also to visit the Night Club; only then shall I know whether I am really losing my sensitivity to autumn. But at least in the Night Club I shall be able to experience again the oak panels and the reflections in the bar's mirror. I wonder whether, one day, I could list such elements in order of importance. I might find then that the Night Club is more important than the Bridge. Naturally, the Bridge is clearer in my mind; but as autumn is a season of the indirect, the allusive, I might find that it is the landscapes I recall with just a wisp of enthusiasm that are central to my sensitivity to autumn.

But once recalled, might not the landscapes then lose their sense of the indirect?

As I step outside, I press the grass with my shoes. It feels like some resilient scrubbing brush.

3

The Night Club is just as I remember: an upper storey room in which tables, chairs and people tower among question-marks of smoke and noise.

I sit at the bar and try to catch a glimpse of an oak panel. It occurs to me that both the panels and the Bridge are of wood. But this is not so surprising, because both are part of autumn. Autumn is the faint, gold thread which, for a short time each year, draws the four walls of my world together. Last autumn at the Conservatory the thread had been the sun on the drinking fountain; tomorrow, if I have not lost my sensitivity to autumn, it might be the sovereign-emblem on my antique sewing machine, or a reflection of gilt in a shop window.

People are looking at me. I wonder whether they think I seem out of place. But perhaps they are just admiring my appearance. Sometimes, after all, I am good-looking, in a conservative way. I certainly wouldn't mind if someone were to make a play for me tonight. It would be appealing to walk to the car with a total stranger, musing on the cold wind and apprehensively contemplating the grey, starless sky. I might even whisper, as I walk, the words to the song 'The Thrill of it All'.

Losing track of my thoughts, I tap an empty cigarette pack. I disapprove of smoking, although I have always been entranced by cigarette cards. Many times in bed I have taken out the collection passed on to me by my aunt and, admiring the cards' church-window colours, allowed myself to drift into reflections of autumn.

The season has such an appealing emptiness! Just a faint alteration in the darkness of the shadows... Just an indefinable desire to transcend rationality with red wine and worn volumes of poetry...

But nothing concrete. Nothing of solidity, of presence.

I rise, and approach the door. I feel sure now that I have not lost my sensitivity to autumn.

4

But as I park the car, I feel a different kind of doubt. I may not have lost my sensitivity to autumn *now* – but suppose when I reach the Bridge it is gone again? I shall have no choice then but to try to forget autumn and its emblems, such as the Bridge. In such an eventuality, the irony would be that at the start of the following year's autumn the mere fact that the season is centred on an awareness of the past (a past that has never really been present!) would result in my being sensitive to the loss of sensitivity I may perceive myself as having this autumn. It would be as though I were falling into an empty passage of misted mirrors, the images of which are the light itself and the spacing of which is a year.

And I am resolved. I shall not go to the Bridge now. Too much depends on it. If I were to lose my sensitivity, a passage of mirrors could wait to supplant the Bridge; and if I were not to lose my sensitivity, the endpoints of the passage, which I just conceived as separated by at least a year, could draw together and trap me the second they become coincident.

I start the car. Tomorrow I shall again visit the Conservatory and the Night Club. These visits will fix the Bridge in my mind. Eventually I shall know so much about the Bridge that I shall be bound to learn how I can keep returning to it only once.

Going Back

As Mark knelt in the sandpit beneath the transplanted flame trees, he peered at the privet hedge surrounding the garden. Twenty years ago he climbed the branches of a similar hedge; twenty years ago he parted sharp twigs to contemplate the house about which he so often made up stories.

Idly, he began to tap the alphabetical blocks the psychiatrists had left him. Although it was night, he could see the blocks clearly: A, C, E, F, G, I, N, P, R, T and U. Close was a toy steamroller, half-buried in the sand.

Gingerly, he felt his arm. His 'recent, adult' memories were supposed to disappear soon but he felt sure they wouldn't. How could a mere drug take away something so rich, so detailed as the record of his life's experiences?

He checked the time. Midnight. Slowly, he drew near the white, stone steps adjacent to the front door. During every December of his childhood a decal of Father Christmas had decorated the door. When arranging the house's reconstruction, however, the psychiatrists had decided against including those objects to which he might respond inappropriately. There was, after all, the danger that he might react to an image of Father Christmas as if it were a divine symbol rather than a past-recapturing one.

He was to visit first the sleepout, which was on the left of the steps. He opened the door, and paused. Even though the sleepout was only one of the rooms in which he had slept, he recalled it well. He could see mosquito coils, like those whose grey, scented smoke had kept him awake on summer nights; he could see a patchwork quilt, like that under which, on winter mornings, he had woken to study his collection of gemstones. He ran his fingers over the quilt, wondering whether he did so from free will or conditioning. The psychiatrists had told him that he had been conditioned to visit each of the house's eleven rooms but he was skeptical. Still, it was degrading that they even thought they could subject a refined person to an experiment. He peered at the painted asbestos walls, wishing that night had not been pronounced the most 'psychologically profitable' time for it. The only light was that of the half moon and the street lamps and it was hard to see clearly.

Clumsily (there was a dresser in his way), he crawled under the bed. Just as years ago, when he played with his toy rocket there, the dust seemed thickest near the skirting-boards. It was disconcerting to realise that the house was only a faithful copy. The Board had spent a great deal. They must consider him worth reclaiming. But then, he had not been just, as they called him, a 'felon'; working by himself he had made important discoveries pertaining to quantum computers; and when the reclamation was complete, and he had approved adult experience and perspectives, he apparently would freely provide his knowledge to the authorities. But did they really believe that by his becoming familiar, in obsessive detail, with childhood objects he would soon become, as it were, a programmable child himself? A *tabula rasa*? The idea was absurd but then, so was the world. That was why fleecing the world had never concerned him.

After ten minutes, the time he was to spend in each room, he left the sleepout. He glanced up. They had even rebuilt the loft. This was really just a recess between the sleepout's ceiling and the roof but the word 'loft' had always seemed right. As a child, he had not entered it: clearly that was why he was not required to enter it now. He started along the verandah, aware of the grey, tongue-like leaves of the century plant and of the rows of transplanted fish fern. Then he opened the door to the lounge.

The lounge was not wholly dark: in the grate were the red cubes of a dying fire. He smiled. He had always loved eating peanuts whilst sitting beside that fireplace. Why had each shell contained only one kernel?

He turned and examined the other side of the room. In the corner farthest from him was a piano and next to the piano was a black, cast-iron magazine rack and an aquarium. Goldfish flashed from one end of the tank to the other; apparently, fish never slept. But the magazine rack had no magazines! Did the psychiatrists want to prevent him from reading? He loved reading. *Treasure Island* was the book that had started him. He had even wanted to be a writer, although his first choice had been to be a concert oboist. If this experiment were not so eccentric, not so certain to fail, he felt sure he would have tried, by now, to kill those responsible. True, the idea of revisiting his old home absorbed him but he had always hated being dominated. But suppose he could be dominated? Were his adult memories vanishing already? No, he had been to the sandpit, then to the sleepout, then to here. He was not an innocent child yet.

When he entered the kitchen, he noticed first the wallpaper, which had fruit motifs. Columns of split oranges and lemons were barely discernible in the gloom. He felt taken aback. It was almost unfamiliar, that wallpaper! His recollection of it must have been deeply submerged. He began to wander around. There were the bright triangular egg-cups, empty. There was the wood stove: its once-silver hot-plates were black. Long ago he had burnt his fingers on it.

Absent-mindedly, he moved towards the bedroom next to the kitchen. He tapped the large cheval mirror on his right. What he remembered most about this room was the high dresser, in which his father had kept his suits. The dresser had always appeared to loom out of darkness. When had he last visited the room? Twenty years ago? Surely not, yet his insurance policy would mature next year.

He entered the adjoining bedroom – and stopped. He could not recall what he was doing. He sat on the bed. Before him was a lamp, the stand of which was decorated with halved shells. On his right was a shaving-mirror; its back presented a river scene. He was reminded of the 'Rivers of the World' series of cigarette cards his father gave him. Of course, the series that appealed to him most was the one showing scenes from pirate stories.

But what was he doing?

In the dining room, he found himself before a large table. He examined it. He had forgotten that yellow, checked motif but the psychiatrists must have taken the information from his memory. Memory... computers. What was a computer?

He sat beside the table. Perhaps one day he could have breakfast here again. Breakfast had always been his favourite meal because it was closest to dawn, his favourite time of day. But why did only cereals have cards? Was cereal, which was supposed to be wholesome, so unpopular that children had to be wooed with cards, special offers and plastic toys? Still, cereal manufacturers put out plastic toys, such as Crater Critters, less often now so perhaps breakfast had become more popular. Or perhaps the little plastic sculptures were now considered too dangerous to present in a cereal context.

As he reached under the table and grasped its steel legs, he began to laugh. To think his whole life had led to this! His friends or peers, if he even had any, were married, settled – but he had always been a loner. That was why he spent so much time playing by himself in the hen run. The halved water tanks there reminded him of ships. He laughed again.

Then he stopped laughing and became aware of the silence.

As soon as he entered the first of the bedrooms adjoining the dining room, he looked around cagily. The room seemed familiar. Had he already visited it? But of course he had. Not long ago his sister had asked him to come in bed with her. She had shown him the face of her watch and stated that it was 'iridescent'. Really, however, it had been merely luminous.

To reach the second bedroom, he had to cross the dining room once more. When he was inside, he hesitated. He had been wandering around for a long while, now: what was he after? Contentment? Security? His super-ball? The darkness frightened him. He opened the curtains. They had pictures of Noah's Ark. He craned towards the sandpit. When he was in it, Mrs Cummings sometimes leaned over the fence and talked to him. His toy cupboard was more fun than the sandpit, though. It was a spaceship. It could fly to Mars or Pluto. He liked hiding in... confounded right-wing government! What were they doing to his mind? Always questions. He grasped his head and closed his eyes.

The bathroom, toilet and laundry could be reached only from outside the house. He reeled through the back door and towards the bathroom. Perhaps tonight was bath night. If it was, where was his toy fish? Perhaps he could go and get it and escape from the bloody Captain Kidd.

In the toilet, he clutched the chain. The floor was wet. Behind was the copper. A box of Cold Power loomed out of the darkness.

He began to stagger along the footpath.

He fell into his sandpit.

A while later, he reached for a brick. Then he gathered them all before himself. Soon, he had made the word 'GUN'. He glanced around. Why was he away from his cabin? Someone might tell the captain. He'd kill them!

He ran into the sleepout, took off his clothes, threw them on to the floor.

Suddenly, he listened. He could hear footsteps. They were heavy.

He edged towards the bed, and lay still.

Presently, the door closed.

I Turn You On

1

I sit on the see-saw and look at the park. The air smells of borewater. The paperbarks make me think of the tissues I used the time Mr Rieder made me cry. He hates making me cry; sometimes it makes him cry, too. The grass is bright green like the lights on the Death Star game in the video arcade.

Mr Rieder comes for me most days. He says he loves me and he certainly likes to talk to me. He talks a lot. He says it's so much better here than where he lives. I don't know where he lives. I don't know much about Mr Rieder except that he used to be a skipper of a tug boat and was born in a place called Friedland. He has a wife called Dorle and a daughter called Gutrune. He says he 'tries to keep them at arm's length'. He is very old, with a red face that always becomes redder as he gets enthusiastic. He wears purple baggy shorts that make his legs look white and a black t-shirt with a smiling face on it. His hair is grey, like the sand under the see-saw. He says he has always liked nine year-old boys.

I see Mr Rieder approaching now. I wonder how I feel. I'm never sure but maybe I'm unsure about that, too. Mr Rieder tells me so much that perhaps I'll learn one day.

"Aidan – how's my special little red-headed angel today?" He gently lifts me off the see-saw and hugs me.

"Hi, Mr Rieder. I'm glad you've come to see me. I need a big man to look after me." I don't know why I said that. I don't know why I've always said that.

"It's normal, Aidan. All boys need a man to turn to – someone they can tell their problems to, someone they can get really close to."

"Yes, Mr Rieder."

He kisses me on the lips and then looks straight into my eyes. "And we're especially lucky because I love you more than anything or anyone in the world."

"Will you always love me, Mr Rieder? Even when I grow up?"

"You never will grow up, Aidan. You'll always be beautiful and new. You'll always be in the park enjoying yourself or having fun in the video arcade or even just lying with me in that Special Room we go to when we want to be really close for a long time."

"I'm so happy that you can give me what a boy needs." I've said this before. I know it pleases Mr Rieder.

He lowers me on to the sand. "Now, what shall we do? Do you feel like leaping around with a ball for a bit? I'll try not to miss your throws! Or do you want to have a yarn about anything that's on your mind? Or do you want to do that special thing we do and leave everything else until we're relaxed? We've got the park to ourselves, as always."

"I'd like to do the special thing, Mr Rieder."

"Then we will, Aidan. I know it's as important to you as it is to me." He beams down at me. Then, he slowly kneels, his face red.

2

In the video arcade, I play the Death Star game. My tongue is between my teeth as I concentrate on the flashing lights. They're bright green, like the grass in the park. I'm scoring much higher than I've ever scored before. I almost hope Mr Rieder won't come and interrupt me. I feel surprised at this thought.

There is warm breath on my neck. "You're scoring really well, Aidan. Don't let me distract you."

It's Mr Rieder, of course. He's wearing white sneakers without socks and the baggy shorts with pictures of what he says are hibiscus flowers. They remind me of the radar dishes in the Mutant Species Invaders game.

"That's all right, Mr Rieder." I glance over my shoulder. "I'm getting really good at this."

"You have a fine mind as well as a stellar personality and that's important. I like to think I have a good mind, too." He draws up a stool and sits beside me. "Did I ever tell you I'm an external student?"

"I think so." My score goes up by another 1000.

"After I retired I decided that I should do something to improve myself. I've always been interested in the arts, literature especially. I used to feel so low driving a tug boat day after day just to earn money for my wife and daughter who don't really love me. I always wanted a son. So I signed up for a class, and now I'm taught all about writing and philosophy and semiotics and literary theory, and I read books like *The Pleasure of the Text*. Yesterday, I learned that reading a text – that means a story – is always a 'new' experience, even when you've read it before. I'm not sure I understand quite what that means! But I don't want to bore you."

"You never bore me, Mr Rieder. I like being with you."

I press the wrong button and the game ends. "Oh, fuck! Just when I was going good!" I feel myself scowling.

Mr Rieder puts a hand on my shoulder. "You can have another go later. You can do anything you like, whenever you like."

I look up at him. "Is that really true?"

"Well, of course! What would you like to do now?"

Suddenly I feel confused. "I don't know. Could I meet Gutrune one day?" I'm not sure why I say this.

"I don't know about that, Aidan. She's not very nice. She looks down on me. I caught her taking money from me once. And I say that even though she's my daughter."

"I'd like to see for myself."

He puts a hand between my legs and rubs gently. "This is what boys like most, Aidan. Don't think about Gutrune. She's irrelevant to our relationship."

I close my eyes, enjoying the pleasant feeling.

"I can feel your little tail responding, Aidan. You know I love… *consuming* your little tail." He draws me close, puts one hand on my hip and with the other gently unzips my fly.

3

The Special Room is the same as it was the last time I was in it with Mr Rieder. I don't remember exactly when that was, although it wasn't a long time ago. I always seem to have been going there or to the park or to the video arcade. Once Mr Rieder said we could go to the seashore when I'm more developed but I'm not sure what he meant by that.

As I wander around the Special Room, I try to work out why it's called Special. It's just a white room, really, with lots of black cushions and purple lights that make your skin look creepy. Mr Rieder says its 'decor is really him'.

There's an archway leading into the Special Room and the door opens. Mr Rieder is naked. His skin has sort of folds in it, a bit like the old newspapers and paper bags in the park.

He hurries over to me. "I've missed you, Aidan." He plants kiss after kiss on me. "You're my whole world. You know that."

"Yes, Mr Rieder." But I manage to place my hands in his way. "Mr Rieder, when can we go to the seashore you told me about?"

"Oh, the seashore." He avoids my eyes. "As I said before, you're not really developed enough for that yet... It's a question of resources..."

"What do you mean?"

"So many questions, Aidan! Are they really necessary?"

"It would make me happy to know the answers, Mr Rieder." I feel pleased with my sneakiness in saying this. I've never been sneaky before.

"Oh." He looks undecided, bites his lip. "You know, Aidan, sometimes we ask questions and when we get the answers we wish we hadn't asked the questions in the first place."

"But the only way I can know that is to ask the questions." I screw up my eyes and pretend to cry. "I feel so unhappy not knowing the answers!"

Immediately, Mr Rieder throws his arms around me. "Don't, Aidan. I'm beside myself when I see you unhappy. I'll answer any question you like."

I pause, suddenly a bit nervous. "Who am I, Mr Rieder? Why is it that I'm always in the park or the video arcade or the Special Room? Where are all the other people?" It all comes rushing out.

Mr Rieder looks sad, as though he's just lost something. I feel guilty and a bit embarrassed.

"Aidan, you're what's known as a 'virtual reality' boy. An 'AI' – that means 'Artificial Intelligence' – simulation. I'm not completely sure what that means myself but what you must remember is that it means you're better than a real boy because you can never grow old or die like me. It sort of means that you're in your own world and only I can come to you from the real world because you were programmed to be exactly what I wanted." He hugs me. "Does that make you feel special, Aidan? It should do."

I feel puzzled. "But why didn't you just go for boys in the real world? You've told me about them sometimes."

Mr Rieder sighs. "In the real world, Aidan, people have strange ideas, especially about what's right and wrong. God is behind it all. You get locked up if you do the things we like with real boys. I don't know why. Some boys do start feeling funny afterwards, but it's society's attitude that does that, all high and mighty. A medical examination of a boy's tail, which involves touching it, doesn't hurt him, after all."

"But if a man knows it could hurt the boy because of society he shouldn't do it, should he?"

Again Mr Rieder sighs. "I suppose so. That's why they allowed AI boys, I imagine. A form of release." He glances at me. "I guess all this has made you terribly unhappy, Aidan?"

I am surprised. "Why should it, Mr Rieder? I'm happy you've shared your thoughts with me. Our world sounds nicer than the real world. Although they can't be all that far apart or we couldn't meet at all, could we?" For some reason I smile.

Mr Rieder starts to cry. "Not far apart? Yes, that's true. You're so wonderful. You always say the right things! But I wish I didn't have to be out in the real world most of the time. Yes, we're so alike, you and I. Maybe we are always together in some way." He grasps my shoulders and looks straight into my eyes. "The wonderful thing is that I can see your mind developing each time I meet with you. The program is supposed to evolve, but

I thought programs were just a kind of written text. Still, from what I've learned and said before, they're supposed to change, too and can even be seen to leap in new and unexpected ways – especially when you get to the end. The 'hermeneutic circle' or 'spiral' – but I don't really follow that...."

4

I stand on the shore, although it's unclear to me how I know it's the shore. I do know that Mr Rieder won't visit me here but that others who are somehow like him are nevertheless aware of me. This makes me feel strong, even stronger than when I had the high score on the Death Star game. I raise my arms to the sun, which is just above the sea. The sea goes on forever. I know from what Mr Rieder said that I'll go on forever, too. I also know that in a way I can go almost anywhere now, not just to the park or the video arcade or the Special Room. I step down to the water and look at my reflection breaking apart and joining together as the waves fold in and spiral about my feet.

Open to the Sky

1

"Can't you think of anything but sex?" Sue banged a cup on to the sideboard but her green eyes were more joking than accusing.

Paul folded his arms and smiled. "Well, what else is there?"

"Those vast aisles of radio telescopes just beyond the gates, for a start! We still don't know how far they go."

"I doubt we ever will. I think the gates will always be sealed." He stood and went to the bay windows. Drawing the white lace curtains – Sue had chosen them because their delicate seahorse emblems seemed to complement the sound of the omnipresent breakers – he craned towards the telescopes. The dish of the closest one was pointing, open to the sky, at right angles to his line of sight, its lustrous white support-column bright in the dawn freshness. He wondered what the astronomers were observing, if, of course, there were any astronomers. Sue and he had never seen any and the apparent location of the twin lines of telescopes on an isthmus or headland meant the only access would be through the gates. Perhaps the telescopes would be redundant once the astronomers had achieved their objective, whatever it was.

Sue joined him. Apprehensively, she squeezed his arm, rested her head against his neck. "How did we end up like this?" she said quietly. "Not so long ago you and I were enough for each other. But now..."

Paul was soothing. "It's not our fault. Blame the human condition. The drive for sex with fresh partners is stronger than anything. With us, the sex impulse died out. At least our open relationship means we're still together." He gently turned her head towards him and looked her straight in the eyes. "When we're both old it will be different. There will be no sex to get in the way, and it will be just you and me again, the way it was." He forced a brightness into his voice. "On the subject of which, do you have anyone lined up for today?"

Sue smiled sardonically. "No. It's the old story. People don't seem to like redheads."

"Why, I can't think. You're young and beautiful. Positively dishy." His eyes twinkled.

"Thank you. So are you." Her smile now was unaffected. "Don't ever cut off that beautiful long hair of yours. When you stand near the window it looks like gold."

"If not gilt." He shrugged. "And you know I never do anything without considering you."

"So have *you* anyone lined up for today?"

"Oh, that air-head Donna said she'd call later. I might go with her if I feel up to having to look at that blank expression for hours at a time."

"Well, just let me know when you want me to give you some space."

"What will you do?"

"I might go down to the gates again and see if I can work out one more time how to get access to the telescopes." Idly, she went to the glass top table in the centre of the white-brick lounge and toyed with the roses she had bought the previous day. The petals, like cupped hands, were paper white. Most of the items in the room were white; it was her favourite colour.

"Well, I admire your persistence. I consider it an achievement that we can actually see the ocean, without wondering how to get access to its domain."

The phone rang. Paul hastened towards it, picked up the receiver. "Hi? Donna?" He put his hand over the receiver, and whispered, "It's Donna."

Sue nodded, and pointed towards the front door.

2

As Sue approached the gates, she wondered why she was so captivated by the telescopes. She could see three, the one closest to the gate towering over her. Its support column was smooth like the enamel of a sea-shell. It looked delicate. As on previous occasions, she felt apprehensive that it might actually keel over and crush her. But there was no unfamiliar *whirr* of machinery, no ominous sound of weakening metal – although she told herself that today the sound of the breakers would disguise virtually any sound.

The gates were kelp-yellow and far too high to climb. They were the central portion of a barrier that stretched right across the dunes, in both directions, to the skyline. She put her eye to the seam where the gates met, but as usual she could make out nothing. There was not even an indication as to whether or not they were bolted.

On an impulse she looked back along the road. Their house was a tiny white triangle partially obscured by the mirages and heat haze. She couldn't remember how long she and Paul had been living there. It seemed to have been forever. She was surprised that he was able to draw so many women – and, sometimes, men – out to such an isolated part of the hinterland. No, she wasn't surprised. Paul was beautiful. He was slim and twenty-two and had eyes the colour of summer shadows. So dazzling was his presence that the time before she knew him seemed likewise a mirage. Had she dreamed it? That she had met him late one afternoon rising wet and wild-haired from a dark reef? Whatever, her great fear was that it would eventually all prove to be an illusion and she would one day find herself alone once more, crying into the sunset. True, since they decided on an open relationship they had become closer in many ways and it was also true that she enjoyed casual sex now and again – but there was such danger. Such shadow.

A tiny dust cloud further obscured the house: no doubt Donna had arrived in her Ford. She glanced at her watch. Eight. With any luck Paul would be finished in half an hour and she would be able to go home.

She leaned back against the gate and closed her eyes. The white sand was warm and comforting.

3

"I don't believe this." Sue grasped his arm. "Please tell me this isn't real." She could hear her voice shaking, and it infuriated her. Violently she tensed her arms and legs so that they wouldn't tremble. "Four hours I waited, and now this!"

Paul sat beside her, squeezing her hand. "I'm so, so sorry. I truly am. But I can't help it. It's been welling up for a while but I thought it would pass. I just seem to have fallen for Donna. Believe me, it wasn't my intention."

"I *told* you it was a mistake to see the same person more than once!"

"And you were so, so right! Look, maybe it's just a crush. Can you bear with me until I know?"

Sue closed her eyes, shook her head. "Is it really up to me? I'm obsessed with you." She looked up in alarm. "You don't want me to move out, do you? I mean, we get on so well."

"Of course not. As far as I'm concerned, this place is yours."

"So *you're* going...?" She felt suddenly cold.

Paul said nothing. He went to the window, and then faced her. "How were the telescopes today?" he asked with a forced brightness.

"Just as always." All at once, she burst into tears. "Oh Paul, this is a disaster! This whole place is us, it can't just end with a wave goodbye." She sobbed, great retching sobs. Little lenses of salt water glittered on the glass table.

Paul eased her out of her chair. His voice had a seriousness. "Let's go for a walk. We'll see things more clearly outside."

Silently, she nodded acquiescence.

4

The gates were open.

Sue stared open-mouthed at Paul, her anguish momentarily forgotten. "The gates! Am I...? God – was it Donna?"

Paul was equally taken aback. "I suppose all we can do is go and see."

"But the telescopes seem to go on forever! And how are they supported? The path is so narrow!"

Numbly, she began to follow him. Space-black mussels punctuated the limestone boulders that formed the foundation of the path.

When they had been walking for a few minutes, she inquired apprehensively, "Do you think this alters things?"

"You mean between me and Donna? It's hard to say. I'll admit it's a shock that suddenly our whole world has changed."

She could see that he was just being gentle and that the issue of him and Donna remained as it was. He would never weaken. If only he weren't so considerate and so beautiful, she told herself, she could hate him and free herself!

She managed, "Do you think we should go back?"

Paul shrugged, and turned. Immediately she heard him make an unidentifiable sound.

She turned as well – and felt herself gaping.

The shoreline and the radio telescopes were gone.

Wholly bewildered now, she looked ahead once more. But the path still continued into the sea. It was only just above the water line. If there had been any waves there would have been the danger of their being washed away. It was as though they were in the middle of the ocean.

For some reason, Paul had resumed walking. Was he increasing his pace? And was the sea becoming a little turbulent?

She tried to catch up with him, but the path was treacherous. "Paul, the waves are breaking over the path! Be careful. There could be sharks."

"There's no danger." His hair was wild and in all directions like the quills of a lionfish.

Sue looked down at her feet. The path was below the surface now, although she could still see its whiteness clearly. The water was cold around her calves. Apparently the path had a gentle slope. Why hadn't they noticed before, when they set out? It surely would have been obvious if they had paid more attention to what they were doing. "I'm going back!" she called suddenly. She scrabbled on to the wet concrete. "Paul!" She cupped her hands around her mouth.

But Paul was already wading. Dazedly she watched as his shoulders disappeared below the swell, his head all at once resembling nothing more than a tangle of seaweed from some dark reef.

And then it, too, was gone.

Sue stared at the turbulent swell for a few moments, and then threw herself on to the path, beating with her hands at the orbits of her eyes.

Dreams Never End

1

I stand on the dune and stare out to sea. It is late afternoon and the skyline is shimmering but although this could be due to the heat it is more likely due to the fact that at the horizon begins the next Dream.

I wonder what Dream it will be. The present one is fairly prosaic: I descend from the dune and start to walk along the great arc of empty shore. My hair is long, and occasional fingers of wind flick bleached and frayed strands across my eyes. At such moments I try to determine how long I have been on the Dream Islands. My skin is very tanned, almost umber, so I must have been here for a long time. On the other hand time has no absolute significance on the Islands. Indeed, little has significance here, and almost everything changes. All that remains constant is my knowledge that I must cross Dream after Dream after Dream, trying to find the place where the Dreams correspond with the real world. I reason that there must be such a place, for the number of permutations of landscape, although vast, is finite, and eventually one of these permutations will be indistinguishable from the real world. And by Leibniz's Principle of Indiscernibles this will mean that such a Dream *is* the world.

Absently, I turn. My footsteps follow the curve of the shore, diminishing at the limit of my vision to a row of dots. They make me think of an ellipsis. There is dry wrack, and bleached seashells like little full moons, but there is no indication that anyone else is here or, indeed, has ever been here. It is the same in most of the Dreams. In some of the ocean Dreamscapes I allow another person to walk with me for a while but the focus is always on my solitude. I wonder at my lack of loneliness. Maybe there are Dreams where I am lonely but this is not one of them. My overwhelming emotion is of restlessness, a desire to fulfill my destiny. And a transcendence: I feel powerful.

I kneel by the sea and raise my arms in supplication – to what, I don't know. A strange music, like the panoramic section close to the beginning of Liszt's first Hungarian Rhapsody, is somehow threaded in the landscape itself. I realise that I would not be sad to die beside this infinite sea.

Nevertheless, I start to walk over the ink-coloured waters in the direction of the next Dream.

2

And I am Meren, and my domain is Ocean Below. I shade my eyes from the saffron blaze of the tropical sun, and crane up through the eel-like creepers and the waterfalls and the red-berried bushes to discern Haven and Ocean Above.

Two oceans – one on the summit of a vast plateau, one the receptacle for its tumbling turquoise waters. Ocean Below extends over the entire world but Haven, I know, is somewhere in Ocean Above, perhaps on one of its islands. But I've never visited these islands and I've never met Haven. I can't even be sure he exists.

Yet I envisage myself climbing the mountain to Ocean Above and swimming out to an island black and white with oyster shells and the silt and salt of evaporated seawater. I envisage myself sitting with Haven and staring towards the sunset and the vast volcanic basins that form Ocean Above.

Sunset-coloured fish scribble the seawater in a chaos of bubbles and disturbed sand as I push against the lip of one such volcano and project myself underwater. The water is unexpectedly cold but in this oneiric archipelago the unexpected is not surprising. I think of rock pools and gene pools; of schools of fish and schools of thought, but one thought eludes me: the thought expressing exactly how many times I've crossed this

Dream landscape. I simply can't remember. In many Dreams the shortest distance between two points is not always a line and a line, reciprocally, does not always join two points.

There is an undercurrent that feels like the pushing together of two magnets' matching poles, but I draw myself from it and on to an exposed rock the shape of a shark's fin. Then I wait, not quite sure what to do. In some Dreams I call to Meren and there seems to be a conversation:

"I don't think I'm worthy to follow you."

"I think you are. *I* fall short."

"We must return soon."

"Not through Ocean Below."

"We'll be taking Ocean Above with us. That's where you're wrong. We can never be changed now."

More often, though, there are simply ambiguous words, sentences ('I'm not with you'), or vague tales of even vaguer exploits. Such vagueness usually marks the entrance to another Dream, another isle ('I'll') of the association.

3

A centuries-old ruin at Christmas in some world's southern hemisphere, and a character, who could be myself. His thoughts return continually to the summer water-table in the grey sand far below him.

Perhaps the ruin is close to the sea. The knowledge that below the ruin there is sand supports the conjecture, but the rule in this Dream is that the gaze must always be directed inward, never towards the great sweep of oceanscape that may lie in the opposite direction.

I stand and stretch myself. I am searching for a small notebook - a notebook crumpled and yellow - that I concealed somewhere here last Christmas. Beneath the Christmas water-table, perhaps. I have not left the ruin since hiding the notebook. Indeed, I may never leave the ruin - or, at least, the moment of my leaving it may be forever indefinite, obscure.

I remember neither the words of the notebook (except that I wrote them) nor why I chose to hide it. Such lapses of memory are also part of the logic of this Dream.

I tap the wall closest to me. Next to a hearth, it comprises squall-grey seashells cemented with something that resembles limestone, but it feels surprisingly hollow. I pick at it; a powdery mass comes apart in my fingers, revealing a depression.

I reach into the shadows, cool like the air of an underwater cave: and my fingers grasp the notebook. Strangely lightheaded, I open it.

4

A Dream of reflection. I sit back and read what I have written. There are only a few pages but there is the impression that for every page of writing there are concealed volumes: volumes forgotten, volumes erased, volumes dreamed. There is also a sense of convergence – that written text, Dream and my own situation become virtually indistinguishable, with accounts of the sea blurring with accounts written by the sea.

But if this is the case, who am I?

I go to the window and hold the first page against the pane. It is as though the written characters, the lists of words, are physical objects existing far beyond an exceptionally lutulent glass. The impression is highlighted by the fact that the driftwood-like scrawls on the page resemble the pieces of actual driftwood which, I observe, have been cast by some storm on to the shore.

I allow my eyes gradually to close, gradually to lose their focus.

Dreams do end, but only if we arbitrarily call them 'texts'. Or reality. I open the window and allow the air to receive my pages.

Razorshell

1

Margaret decides not to buy oysters. She tells herself she may not even go to Coles. But then she feels guilty. Isn't she *obliged* to eat oysters? Isn't it her duty to put herself in a sexual mood so that she can be 'fruitful and multiply', as Father Andiamo recommends?

She wanders listlessly around the kitchen. Through the window she can see the children's playground across the street. The large slide reminds her of the mathematical integration sign that her son Wayne had wanted her to explain the other night.

She doesn't like oysters very much. Except for Oysters Kilpatrick, they taste like gritty mucus, slipping coldly down her throat and into her stomach. There to turn into shit. And if she eats oysters she'll feel really horny. She'll want to seize her husband, Bill, as soon as he comes home from his irregular shift and throw him on the bed. And then she'll feel drained. There are higher pursuits than sex anyway. Her patchwork quilt, for example, is still unfinished. The seams.

She pauses to pick up her Bible. Someone put it on her pile of cookbooks by mistake. Or perhaps she put it there herself when she was writing the shopping list, or trying to stop Patty from taking the sharp oyster shells (and bean cans and bones!) out of the kitchen tidy.

Weary, she opens the volume. Its pages are torn. Father Andiamo, who is black-and-white about everything and who has never seen Patty, told her again yesterday that people must be fruitful. He had added that opportunities to improve fruitfulness must be seized, that failure to do so is a sin. Father Andiamo is always producing pearls of wisdom, she tells herself, smiling sadly. But he had not referred explicitly to oysters. Is that relevant?

No, she decides, it isn't. Everyone is aware that oysters are an aphrodisiac. Even snails – known in folk recipes as 'wallfruit'– are supposed to increase the sexual appetite. Absently, she runs her fingers over the edge of a page of the Bible. It is sharp. Are razorshells a kind of oyster?

"The world is my oyster but it's only a shell," she sings softly, remembering Bryan Ferry's 'A Song for Europe'. Suddenly resolved, she tosses the Bible into the kitchen tidy. She knows from experience that the most insignificant biblical instruction soon leads to impossible commands. And then something must give. Kneeling, she takes from the cupboard beneath the draining board a large red capsicum. Tonight for dinner there will be no oysters, just spaghetti bolognaise. She thinks of the white spaghetti snaking among the rich red sauce and feels her guilt receding into the distance.

2

"I want you to wear protection tonight."

Her husband pauses, halfway through peeling off a sock. "What was that?"

"I want you to wear protection tonight." Edgy, Margaret turns away, not wanting to see fixed on her the two apparently lash-less, watery eyes that remind her of oysters.

"A condom?" His voice is sharp. "I don't have one! Father Andiamo believes…"

"I'm not interested in what Father Andiamo says. I only know I don't want any more infants tearing around the house in nine months' time, wrecking everything. I'm fed up with being a doormat, hiding from my feelings." She starts to toy with the knot on her slip.

"You can't cope, can you? Or you're crazy. I've suspected as much for weeks. You have no right to refuse me my rights as a husband. Next you'll be talking about abortion!"

116

Margaret mechanically sweeps from her forehead a few strands of fairy-floss hair. She has long abandoned the idea of coaxing the hair into a recognisable style. "I'm not refusing your rights. All I'm doing is telling you that I want to prevent conception tonight." She closes her eyes, thinking, in spite of herself, of what Father Andiamo would say if he knew.

"And I suppose you have condoms ready for me?"

"Not exactly." She swallows and then takes from the bedside table a piece of cling wrap. "You can wrap this round and over and secure it with an elastic band."

3

It is breakfast time. The container of Stork margarine reminds her of a tombstone. Wayne has left for school, Bill isn't down yet and she is at the mercy of Patty and her three other preschoolers. Already the Just Right has been tipped on the floor and swept up but Patty has now emptied onto the mat a whole bowl of stewed apple. The patch is the shape and colour of a cloud at sunset, except that this cloud won't become diffuse.

She examines Patty with a numb detachment, wondering at the blankness in an infant's eyes. Even when they smile, she tells herself, they're empty. It's hardly surprising a distinction is drawn between infanticide and murder. She picks up the bread knife, glances at its scalloped edge. Puts it down again.

A rhythmical sound makes her look in the direction of Patty's highchair. She leaps up. "Patty! *No!*"

Patty, exploiting the fact that her highchair has slightly uneven legs, is rocking it from side to side. Margaret rushes towards her, staggering as she slips on the apple. She catches hold of the table cloth, the items of which are swept on to the floor just as there is a *crack!*

The highchair has tipped over. Patty is sprawled on the ground, blood coming from somewhere.

Numbly, Margaret kneels over her, fingers groping for the infant's carotid.

The pulse is faint but regular. She feels a relieved disappointment.

Beside Patty is the knife, slippery with blood. Almost without thinking, Margaret aligns the point of the blade with the infant's throat. Then she closes her eyes and presses.

4

"You *cunt*!" Her husband is sobbing at her. "You've *murdered* our baby daughter. You cunt!"

Margaret is almost relieved to be called a cunt because she is now able to produce genuine tears. She lifts her head out of her hands and faces her husband. "How can you do that? How can you think of accusing me of infanticide?"

"Infanticide?" He stares at her, his face now wildly blank. "You cold, hard cunt! Who but a cunt would use a word like 'infanticide' instead of 'murder'?"

"We've been through this before." She tries to speak evenly. "Patty tipped over the highchair. She must have fallen on the knife. I…"

"I can see it in your eyes that you attacked her! Do you hear me? I can see it!"

"Now look, Bill…" Margaret feels a vague apprehension as she sees a figure stalking towards her that looks a bit like her husband. She backs into the kitchen, feeling her way with one hand, trying to keep the figure back with the other.

"Shut your fucking mouth! Do you know what I'm going to do? I'm going to ring the police!" He looks wildly around, then his gaze locks on her once more. "But first I'm going to give you a hiding, you *cunt*!" He seizes a plastic spatula, shoves her on to the floor and starts to lash her legs with the spatula's edge.

The pain is so blinding that Margaret can't even cry out. In panic, she knocks over the kitchen tidy. Margarine containers and capsicum seeds tip on to her, her hair and oyster shells. Trying to protect herself, she scrabbles for a shell just as the figure pushes her on to her back, hands around her throat.

And then somehow she is standing, staring at the object spread out on the floor in front of her. Sticking out of one of its eyes is the round, black end of an oyster shell.

He's dead, she realises. And she's guilty of murder. Not just infanticide.

Or abortion.

Or preventing conception.

Or failing to stimulate her sexual desire with oysters.

But at least it is easier to do her duty now. She slides the shell from the bony circle of her husband's eye and tips it so that she can sip the salty liquid.

The Tulpa

1

"Why you don't just give this guy a hiding if he's causing you so much embarrassment?" Roman stares at his glass of champagne as though doing so might somehow change its vintage. Then he taps the base of the glass smartly with one finger, giving rise to a volley of bubbles.

Michael gestures testily. "There's this thing called the law. If you go around giving people hidings you tend to get locked up or, what's possibly worse, subjected to counseling!"

"But you don't really mean you believe in the possibility of elementals?"

"Not elementals, tulpas. They're from Tibetan philosophy and folklore. A western translation is 'thought form'. Similar, I suppose, but not exactly like memes. About a hundred years ago one Alexandra David-Néel claimed to have created a tulpa in the form of a monk, just by concentrating on physical and mental details. It became quasi-autonomous and even tried to kill her before it could be deconstructed – although that was apparently quite an undertaking. Tulpas frequently become vindictive in this way, so the story goes, trying to supplant their creators."

"You must really have a down on this guy if you're prepared to sic one on to him, scare him to death."

Michael takes from his suit a mass of notes and waves them in Roman's face. "Godfrey Rieder is a piece of low life. These are notes on him I've made and I'll use them when I construct the tulpa. Every relevant fact pertaining to him and his behaviour is down here. I know everything about his appearance and background. Go on, ask me something."

"What colour are his eyes?"

"A pale dun sort of shade. Like that champagne you insist on not drinking, actually."

Hastily, Roman drains his glass. "How tall is he?"

"One hundred and eighty centimetres exactly. His nose is blunt, his features chiseled. His weight is precisely 100 kilograms, he measures 60 centimetres around the waist and wears XL size t-shirts, which are always red and have the logo of some whisky company. He has size nine feet. In his office, where he works on the fifth floor as a purchasing executive – he's trying to get a seat on his company's board – he always wears either a charcoal suit or a maroon one."

"And why do you have a down on him?"

"Because he stole Mimi from me. And now he's treating her like a piece of nothing!" Michael glances at him with scorn. "As you damn well know. Are you trying to get me going?"

"No, no. I wouldn't dream of it. Just let me know if the plot succeeds."

"It will succeed fantastically. Rieder will be called to account. Fortunately he has a death wish, so his behaviour won't have to be altered much."

2

Later that evening, Michael slowly makes his way to the lounge, absently sits in his maroon vinyl settee. He is less certain now that he is by himself. Even if tulpas are physically possible and not just folklore, he wonders, can he form something that is supposed to require decades of contemplation of Tibetan philosophy? Still, perhaps his knowledge of Idealist philosophy will be sufficient and all he has read suggests that the Tibetan theory corresponds to familiar Idealist themes, such as Berkeley's view that reality comprises ideas in the mind of God.

"And I'm godlike," he tells himself, standing before the hearth-mirror and straightening his tie. He is in his mid-twenties and 'upwardly mobile', as they used to say. His body is toned; his eyes are wide-spaced and the colour of the summer sky; and his hair, swept casually above his right temple, is blond where the sun has caught it. How could Mimi possibly break with him and fall in with Godfrey Rieder? He feels all at once wildly incensed – and then feels pleased that he is incensed. He suspects that intense emotion will be a key element in the construction and, perhaps, testing of the tulpa.

But what will give the tulpa being? Surely merely concentrating on physical and mental attributes won't be enough to make it exist? Surely some kind of rigid framework will be needed to ensure there is coherence?

He takes out the notes he waved at Roman. Every ingredient is there, it's true, but as unlinked details only. He will need to join them together.

A story. He will write a story with himself as character. That will concretise exactly what he's after. Then he'll post it on the 'net and make sure Rieder sees it. His fear on reading the story will serve to focus the tulpa on him.

And, he tells himself, to make sure of this focus, he'll call the story itself 'The Tulpa'.

3

Godfrey leans back in his chair, puzzled and a little worried. The email from Mimi this morning was right. Someone *has* posted on the firm's website an attack on him. But who is responsible? The name on the story, Daniel King, is obviously a penname (although didn't he once read a story called 'Semi-Detached' by someone called that?). No one would risk a libel suit by linking himself to such an attack in the public domain. Michael Styles is the obvious culprit – but should he take the story's tulpa idea seriously? He only skimmed the first part of the story. Maybe he should have read more....

He concentrates. The office is absolutely quiet and he wonders whether this should concern him. But the quiet is not remarkable, given that everyone has gone home. Indeed, he reflects, quietness may even be a blessing. Presumably a thought-form – if such an absurd thing is even possible – would, if it were in the building and wanting to attack him, make some kind of noise.

Nevertheless, he continues to feel worried.

He gets up and looks out of the window. The city lights and a few bright stars are like the negative of one of the join-the-dots puzzles he used to distract himself with as a child. He finds himself staring first at one line of lights and then another, making up different patterns at whim. But then the darkness of the buildings seems to thrust itself forwards, destroying the patterns which, he realises, are after all only in his mind anyway.

He wonders whether he should attempt a reconciliation with Styles. He could give Mimi the push, be blunt with her. He had only enticed her away from Styles for the hell of it. She's an attractive woman, there's no doubt about that, but her incessant whining and social climbing (when she's not acting like some sixty year-old!) are starting to become a real trial. Moreover, he's sure she's been secretly following him lately and that could be a great inconvenience given that he's hoping to score with the new Accounts secretary in the near future. He thinks fondly of the Accounts secretary, the way she has recently been paying him compliments. She's bubbly and not too smart: just the type of girl he finds appealing. He can't stand those who always demand security and expect him to lead a monastic existence.

But dumping Mimi would be too much of a concession to Styles. He doesn't want the man to lord it over him, after all. It is important that he be kept at a distance. He had broken off reading his incoherent story for precisely this reason.

Still, it might be advantageous to know how the story ends. And perhaps 'Daniel King' gives some clues as to his real identity or at least describes the tulpa and how he is supposed to be attacked.

Deciding to bring the webpage back up, he returns to his desk – and the power goes off. He feels an alarmed annoyance and then a sinking feeling as he realises that if the power doesn't come on within five minutes the security failsafe will cut in and he won't be able to get out of the building until the following morning.

And then Mimi will think he's spent the night with the Accounts secretary.

He'll go to the ground floor. Maybe he will be able to attract the attention of a passerby and get him or her to ring the after-hours security number. Relieved that he is wholly familiar with the layout of his office but irritated that the building's designers had apparently scorned the idea of something as simple as a key, he picks his way in the direction of the fire escape. Occasionally, he pauses, listening (and feeling embarrassed as he does so) for any noise that might indicate the presence of the tulpa.

But everything is quiet.

Soon he is descending the cold, unswept, concrete throat that is the stairwell of the fire escape. It has the dry smell that concrete always does, and its dust makes him think of the ash of an old hearth. A few minutes later, the familiar handle of the ground-level door is in his hands. Quickly, he draws it open and he is in the foyer.

With a rising hope he perceives that there are people in the street. He hurries over to the door, pounds on the glass. "Hallo! I'm trapped in here! Can anyone do anything?" He glances behind, hoping that the noise hasn't attracted anything towards him; again he feels embarrassed that he should even consider such a possibility.

But the glass appears to be too thick to transmit sound and far too thick to be broken. Also, he suddenly realises the dark background is preventing anyone from seeing him anyway.

Absently, he returns to the stairwell and begins to lumber up the fire escape once more.

As soon as he is back in his office, he wonders what to do. He is resigned to spending the night in the building now but he knows he'll never be able to sleep. He'll be far too apprehensive, and he's never been able to sleep in chairs or on the floor anyway. And he can't even make a cup of tea, let alone have a whisky, which he really needs! Almost beside himself, he sits on his desk – and his hand jars against his telephone. He nearly faints with relief. How idiotic of him not to consider ringing in the first place!

He picks up the receiver but again something is wrong. There's no dial tone. The line is dead. He thinks of his mobile.

It is in his drawer, but he remembers that its battery gave up around four o'clock and he doesn't have his charger with him.

He forces himself to think clearly. He could use his laptop to send an email to Mimi, tell her of his predicament. She may not check her email until the following morning but at least if she notices the time on the email she will have demonstrable proof that he was available then and not with the Accounts secretary.

Put out that no one he knows checks email at night – they're too busy getting drunk – he turns on the laptop. As soon as there is the light of its softly-glowing characters (like the glitter of a Christmas tree in the dark), he connects to the 'net.

He is taken aback. For some reason his startup page has become the one with the story about the tulpa! Quickly, he begins to read, and sees that it describes him trapped in this very office, with no power. Worse, he is informed not only that he will be unable to send any emails but also that he will be unable to set off the fire alarm to attract attention or, indeed, make any kind of stand.

"Not while I'm still here!" Determined, he brings up the Hotmail page, enters his username and password.

Nothing happens. The page just hangs.

He hits the backspace on his laptop's keyboard and reads in the story that the page just hangs.

Almost sick with fear now, he debates whether he can steel himself to read the rest of the story. But there are only a few more sentences – and suppose they describe something ghastly happening to him? All at once, he regrets everything he has done: his meanness in stealing Mimi from Michael; his unremarkable life-focus, his naive distractions. What a mistake not to have sought a more engaging, a more insightful vision. The possibilities must surely always have been there, waiting to be realised.

Really, he tells himself – and he is aghast at the thought, although another part of him is skeptical that it is even possible – the most appropriate outcome would be for him to die.

He glances out at the city lights once more. The door leading to the balcony is double, like the boards of some open, transparent book. He finds himself unaccountably drawn towards it and the abyss of the night. He tries to fight the attraction, make himself rigid, but it is as though something (his subconscious? surely not the tulpa?) has seized him.

Now he is on the parapet. As he feels himself being made ready to push himself over, he experiences a numb surprise to find that there is no accompanying fear, just satisfaction – as though finally his existence has achieved meaning, finally his existence has point.

Chat Room

1

"Have you considered that this chat room bully may be just messing about?" Harry takes a piece of toast from the rack, tosses it into the air in the way that always amuses Dot, and catches it deftly on his side plate. Then he reaches enthusiastically for the jar of pear jam. "Mmm! Nothing is better than toast and pear jam. It's sweet without being sickly."

"No, he really does try to attack me. About the only thing he's got going for him," she passes Harry the butter knife, "is that he gives reasons for his views." For once, Harry's trick does not even make her smile. In her still-full mug of tea, the reflection of her knitted brows makes her think of a broken stick. "Why do you ask?"

"Because, my innocent beauty – or should that be beautiful innocent? No matter – the 'net is all about illusion. Nothing is as it seems. Half the web pages you read are little more than fiction."

"I know, I know." Suddenly, she smiles. "At least I've got you. Sometimes when I'm in front of the computer screen for hours, staring at all those funny characters made up of tiny dots, I feel that reality's an illusion and I'm about to see right through it. But at least I can believe in you. You never irk me."

"Indeed. Would you like me to do my toast-tossing trick again?" He laughs and then checks the time. "I still don't know why you don't just forget about the chat room if this guy bothers you so much."

"It's a matter of principle. He mocks everything I say. I could strangle him, stab him, beat him over the head!"

"It's the chat room called Rock and Roll Hits and Stars of the Sixties, isn't it? I've seen you when you're logged in. It always amazes me how quickly you can type."

"That's the one. And the guy – he uses the nick 'Aleph-Zero' – keeps butting in on my conversations. Yesterday his dogma was that the only band worth listening to is Pink Floyd."

"Well, I don't mind them myself. Their *Meddle* album...."

"Yes, but at least you don't make out that everyone who disagrees is daft! He's always making personal attacks. Just because I said I like Gerry and the Pacemakers, he said I probably need one."

"What? A Gerry?"

She swats him with the newspaper. "No! A pacemaker! I let slip not long ago that I've just turned forty-nine and now he keeps harping on about my age." Self-consciously, she tries to examine her reflection in the bright metal of the teapot. But its dimpled surface means she can see only the most general features of her face: the lifeless, though still blonde hair; the determined, though not angular, chin; the slightly droopy eyelids. "And when I mentioned I love pizza, he said it was just glorified cheese on toast. With politics, I said I vote for the Greens, and he said 'any ideology that permits everything, thereby permits ideas leading to its own destruction'. He's even a climate change skeptic! I didn't begin to follow that argument and I'm not sure why I even tried but he said something about the 'climate change hypothesis' not being 'falsifiable', whatever that means. Yes, I really could strangle him!"

"Don't strangle me then because I incline towards those views, too!"

"That's different. You're you and I love you. Anyway, Tracy – you know, my computer whiz pal from my uni days – said a while back that she may be able to track him down."

"Well, be moderate, O one to whom I'm deeply attached. Don't do anything silly." Harry stands, beams and then draws her head towards his lips, which he kisses. "I'm going to work now to earn my pennies. Our firm is developing some new insurance products and I've got to ensure there's liaison with the proper regulatory bodies."

She nuzzles against his neck. "I never even knew your finance company was involved in insurance. We've been married nine years and I'm still learning new things about you, you fantastic man."

"Ah, retaining a certain mystery is the secret of what you'd call a 'phenomenal' relationship! Now don't let this Aleph-Zero character get to you. If you do, I'll be home to hide all the sleeping tablets and razor blades."

"I may not even log on. I'll clear up here, do a bit of housework and only log on if I feel bored."

2

It is nine in the morning and Dot is in the lounge. For a minute or so, she arranges a cut-glass vase of pink Iceland poppies on a doily. Then the doily suddenly catches her attention. "Little pieces of nothing joined together with paper," she murmurs. Then, with an almost masochistic feeling of foreboding, she manoeuvres the black vinyl chair in front of the desk with the computer terminal and printer, checks that she has a clear view of the screen and turns the power on. After the usual seconds of computer noise, which always makes her think of someone vacuuming in a typing-pool, the icons appear and she double-clicks on one for an IRC client. Rows of characters whiz from the top of the screen to the bottom. Seconds later she sees that she is connected to the server.

Who else is online at the moment? She brings up the task bar, leans forward. The usual bots, she sees, plus SignSystem – he's always good for a nostalgic yarn – Humdinger (he doesn't ring a bell); BeautyIsOnlySkinDeep; and, of course, Aleph-Zero. She begins to type.

<DotE> Did anyone see the programme on Bob Dylan last night? They played quite a few tracks I'd never heard before.

She waits, wondering if she should put on a CD. But then SignSystem replies.

<SignSystem> I saw a bit of it. Are you talking about the Blonde on Blonde sessions?

And then, of course, Aleph-Zero butts in.

<Aleph-Zero> Rob Zimmerman is manure. The simplicity of his melodies is at odds with his songs' lyrical complexity

and allusiveness. The songs end up sounding ironic. In future years, he'll be remembered, if he's remembered at all, simply as someone who caught the spirit of his time.

<DotE> Look, Aleph-Zero, I'm getting really sick of you! Why can't you just find another site? I've half a mind to report you to the moderators!

<Aleph-Zero> On what basis? I've said nothing to get under your skin – today, anyway! I'm entitled to air my views.

<DotE> It's funny how your views are always exactly the converse of mine!

<Aleph-Zero> That's because you follow the herd, Dotty. If I didn't know better, I'd say you were a housewife trying to find some meaning in your wooden life! There's still time, you know. You're not sixty yet, are you? Do you enjoy knitting?

Dot feels a triumphant glee. If Aleph-Zero continues to attack her like that, she really will have ammunition to use against him! The moderators have clear rules about sexism and attacks. He'll be booted off the site, maybe even banned. She tells herself to remain calm, try to draw the pest out.

<DotE> And what's the problem with being a housewife?

<Aleph-Zero> There isn't one. But obviously you don't have the temperament for it. Presumably, though, you dote on your husband so much you're resigned to your plight.

<DotE> Aleph, you zero, I'm going to ignore you and your cracks. SignSystem, I'm not sure what sessions they were. They were about halfway into the program.

<SignSystem> I think I missed that part.

<Aleph-Zero> You're weak, Dotty. You throw in the towel. Did you ever give up smoking, as you intended?

Dot is confounded. She can't remember even mentioning her intention to give up smoking, at least, not to anyone online.

<DotE> How do you know I wanted to give up smoking? In any case it's nothing to do with you!

<Aleph-Zero> A bad memory, too, it would appear. It was when you were enthusing about Spooky Tooth's The Last Puff record. You said you only smoke outside and you got burned up when I replied that you therefore have more respect for your house than for your own lungs.

<DotE> I don't remember that. Go throw yourself off a cliff, Aleph-Zero, you tosser.

<Aleph-Zero> Cliff? Aren't you just The Living Doll!

Dot clicks in exasperation and breaks the connection.

3

As Dot ascends the stairs to Tracy's apartment (she has a fear of lifts), she tries to recall details of her and Tracy's previous conversations about Aleph-Zero. She remembers that Tracy, who works for the state's largest internet provider, told her she could easily help to identify the location of any of the provider's clients, but she can't remember whether she told her if Aleph-Zero is one of them.

Slim Tracy, who is wearing a white linen dressing gown and a towel of similar material around her head – presumably she has just washed her hair – is on the balcony, smoking and looking out at the street.

Dot playfully taps on the flyscreen behind her. "Enjoying the view?"

Tracy starts and turns. "Dot! Come inside, come inside!" She stubs out the cigarette and shepherds Dot into the passage, gesturing to the right as she does so. "How do you like my new print? It's by Seurat. Excuse the dressing-gown – I feel a bit seedy this morning. To what do I owe the pleasure of your company? And how's Harry?"

Dot smiles. "He's my rock." She throws herself on to the couch of Tracy's plush, pink velour suite – she feels as though she's sitting on tightly-packaged fairy floss – and then gestures vaguely. "And I do owe you a visit, Trace. But it's the same problem. That guy who harasses me online all the time. I'm starting to feel trapped."

"Ah, the quest for Aleph-Zero. The last time we spoke, you said you'd consider letting me nose into his personal details for you, even send him a warning if he's one of our clients." She feigns a guilty smile. "I do feel naughty but I've found one fact that might be of use!" She flips a cigarette between her lips, where there are still traces of the previous day's lipstick. "But what the hell!"

133

"I don't remember the bit about the warning but that's really fantastic. Thank you. I knew I could count on you." Taken aback at her loss of memory – surely Aleph-Zero isn't right? Surely she's not getting old? – she lies back and accepts the can of Jack Daniels and cola that Tracy reaches over and passes her. The red rug in front of the couch feels fleecy and warm on the soles of her feet.

"The good news is that Aleph-Zero lives in the same general area as you do – if you can call that good news! But apart from that, I can't narrow things down much, unfortunately. He's not one of our clients, and Lord knows what his angle is, but he has a static IP and that, plus some other tricks I won't bore you with, did help me to get a fair idea of where he is."

"My area, you think." Dot chews her lip and then looks at Tracy. "What do you think that means?"

"Hard to be sure, little canary. But it probably means you know the person in real life."

4

<DotE> Does anyone here have any records by Four Jacks and a Jill?

<RedLetter> Their the band that had a hit with Master Jack, Arent they?

<DotE> Yes, but I actually like their song Penny Paper a whole lot more.

<RedLetter> U mean Penny Lane by The Beatles?

<DotE> No, Penny Paper. The "ba-ba-ba-ba-ba-ba-ba-ba-BAR" bit is fantastic!

<Humdinger> Has anyone ever heard of a bootleg by Gilbert O'Sullivan called D'Oyly Carte?

<Aleph-Zero> Master Jack is a song about control. To control someone you have to know them.

<RedLetter> No, I havent heard that.

<Aleph-Zero> And to know someone you have to share, semiotically, either their physical or their mental space.

<DotE> Aleph-Zero, is there any way to stop you hijacking my conversations? You must be the most unpleasant tosser I've ever come across!

<Aleph-Zero> Oh really? Well, I have an amusing trick that involves tossing a piece of toast. You might like that!

Dot quickly breaks the connection.

5

For almost an hour, Dot merely sits, uncertain what to do, to think. She's not even sure of her emotions, except that she's aghast. Harry and Aleph-Zero! The same person! No, she can't credit it. There's no sense in it. Harry is fantastic and affectionate, while Aleph-Zero does nothing but irk her. Harry would never play such a mean trick.

Nevertheless, Harry himself had told her that he shares Aleph-Zero's views. And it's unquestionable that different characteristics of people emerge in different ways, depending on the context. Also, Tracy provided firm evidence that Aleph-Zero is someone she knows.

But she loves Harry! Almost beside herself, she fumbles for a cigarette, which she quickly lights. What a worthless person she must be, she thinks, to attract such contempt. No, she's a person of infinite worth! She simply hasn't thought carefully enough about how to reply to Harry/Aleph-Zero's statements. As Tracy once said, every argument has a counter-argument; nothing can ever actually be *proved*.

She takes a deep draw of smoke and finds herself remembering all her soul-searching conversations with Harry about giving up smoking, all their shared confidences. Suddenly, she is decided. Harry must pay for his meanness. But what should he do? Nothing extreme, of course – she doesn't want to be locked up – but something that will reveal her final, unquestionable, intellectual triumph over him. Something drawn out, something she can relish.

She has an inspiration. She will log on to the chat room while Harry is with her. She will type the silliest, most vacuous things she can think of and make sure Harry is reading them over her shoulder. She will look up into his face as soon as she has typed them. And no retort will be possible because he can't be Aleph-Zero in her presence!

6

"I wish I never had to hear the words 'insurance' or 'economy' again!" Harry pretends to stagger in. He throws his briefcase on to the occasional table where Dot arranged the Iceland poppies. The vase shakes.

"Insurance and economy. There you are, Harry. The words again. Sorry." Dot smiles sweetly at him and then goes to the computer.

Harry snakes off his tie, directs at her a perplexed expression. "You look a bit cut up. Anything worrying you?"

"No, no. Actually, I thought you might want to see for yourself," she begins to tap at the keyboard, "the Aleph-Zero problem. I'm about to log on to the chat room." She glances at Harry but his face is unreadable. She smiles to herself.

"Well, all right but first I'm going to have a glass of wine. A few clients were sore at me for some reason and I need to chill out. Call me when you're online."

Dot double-clicks on one of the IRC icons. The usual rows of characters fill the screen and then she is logged on. She feels Harry's hot breath on her neck. There is a faint scent of garlic.

<DotE> I was listening to the Monkees today and I think Daydream Believer is the most phenomenal song ever written. The line 'You once thought of me as a white knight on a steed' is better poetry than anything in Shakespeare, in my view.

She looks around at Harry but his expression is still unreadable.

He says, "I suppose you're trying to provoke your pal Aleph-Zero, my love? Maybe you should just make it up with him."

Suddenly, Dot is exasperated. She spins around. "Oh stop all the bull, Harry! I know damn well that *you* are Aleph-Zero!"

"Oh!" Harry draws himself up. Strangely, he appears shocked. He goes to the cabinet, where he left his wine glass. "What makes you think that?" he calls, in a rather affected tone.

"I'm not even going to bother giving you my reasons."

He returns to her side, and points at the screen. "That's probably just as well because I see that Aleph-Zero has already replied."

<Aleph-Zero> Nice try, Dotty. Sorry to disappoint you! But don't try to work out who I am or you may get a further series of shocks!

"Good God!" Flabbergasted, Dot turns on Harry and eyes him with only slightly less accusation. "I don't understand. How is this possible? What's going on?"

Harry shrugs. He drains his glass, turns to put it on the occasional table. Straightens his jacket. Then he looks over her shoulder once more.

<Aleph-Zero> The first shock might be that your Harry notices, for example, that you have *two* chat icons and concludes that *you* are Aleph-Zero and have been having vitriolic conversations with yourself. You've been to uni, after all. Your dumbness could be an act. All very playful and in keeping with theories of the decentred self but it might mean an appointment with the shrink for you, Dotty!

Dot manages, "Harry, you're smart. How does he know all this? Who is he? Is he God?"

Harry gently leads her away from the computer. "There is no God, Dot. They used to call God 'the cosmic author' and I suppose that if this were a text, there would be someone who could intervene, godlike, the way Aleph-Zero is for some reason – maybe to amuse, maybe to create a heightened sense of play, maybe to pull the rug out from under readers' feet. Whatever. But it isn't a text. Thank God is all I can say."

"But the chat room conversation... that's a sort of text, isn't it?"

"True, but this isn't. A philosopher did something similar a long time ago." Harry picks up the vase of Iceland poppies and then lets it fall. Little droplets of water roll like tiny marbles over the carpet. "It's a real object. The 'net doesn't quite dominate our lives yet!"

Dot shakes her head, wholly at a loss. She feels there's some vital reply she should make but for some reason she can't think of what it is, much less articulate it. She glances from Harry to the vase's doily and back again and then closes her eyes.

Catenary

1

"Just a second, please." I put down the bowl of gruel and, after pausing to check my tie in the mirror, go to the door. Through its leaded pane I can see a vague shape.

"Mr King? I represent the Royal Dental Foundation. Are you aware that many people, unable to afford huge dental bills, do not seek treatment for tooth decay, thereby paving the way for all sorts of other health complications?"

The man, who is dressed in a pale green shirt that has been buttoned up the wrong way, thrusts a pamphlet at me.

"No, I didn't realise that." I accept the pamphlet. "But it makes sense. I have very good teeth myself."

"Would you be prepared to make a small contribution?"

"Of course." I reach for my wallet. "How much?"

"Well, that depends on what you can afford."

I count out ten fifty dollar notes. "It's not much I know but I guess it'll help."

The man looks at the money in disbelief. "That's extremely generous of you." He passes me another pamphlet, on which are photographs of decayed teeth like mossy tombstones; then he nods and quickly starts down the drive – presumably before I can change my mind.

I regard the space in my wallet where the fifty dollar notes were. I have contributed to three such foundations this week.

2

As I descend the steps with the bowl of gruel, I hear the sound of chains. Will must be trying to escape again. I am amused. Doesn't he know by now that there's no way out?

"Here you are, Will. I thought you might prefer a bowl of gruel to your usual crust." I narrow my eyes, trying to resolve his shape among the shadows. Unfortunately, he has few distinguishing features and he can barely be told from the sacks and old boxes on the floor of the cellar. He could be anyone.

"Look, why are you doing this to me?" he asks. His throat must be especially dry, for his words sound broken.

"Why am I doing what to you?" I enunciate precisely. Experience has taught me that this helps to block out the chamber's unpleasant smell.

"This!" He tries to spread his arms but the chains drag them down. "This prison! This torture! What have I ever done to displease you?"

I observe him coolly. "Absolutely nothing that comes to mind."

"Then why?"

"Surely you realise by now what sort of place the world is?" I try. "Ultimately, everyone always puts his own interest first."

Will puts his head in his hands. Then he looks up. "You hate me. That's right, isn't it?"

"It's not that. If anything, I am indifferent to you."

"You get pleasure from hurting me?"

I glance towards the cat o' nine tails in corner. "It's not that either."

"Well? What then?"

I contemplate him for a few moments, wondering whether I would extract more anguish by not answering his question. But of course, it is impossible to decide. I shrug, although I know his eyes, almost crusted shut with sores, can barely see me. "It's just that... in some sense your presence is necessary."

"If I ever get free, I'll do the same to you!"

I laugh politely, as I quickly take out my handkerchief and put it over my nose. "I'd expect nothing less."

3

I am a person who enjoys a set routine. Every afternoon at four o'clock, I dress in my fawn suit and freshly polished beige shoes and stroll down to the newsagent for the evening paper. If rain is forecast, I make sure to take my umbrella, which I always keep tightly furled.

As I hand over my coins to the Thai proprietor, I glance at the headlines: 'Carnival disaster kills fifty'. I feel simultaneously nauseous and saddened. I quickly glance elsewhere on the page but the only other story concerns some explosion in a Liberian refinery, which I find equally distressing. Apparently four hundred died. I almost resolve to ask for my money back.

Paper folded under my arm, I start back towards home. The insulators on the power poles are like teeth. As a retired civil engineer in the shipbuilding industry, I know that the curve of a freely-suspended wire is called a 'catenary'. Birds arc around the box trees that line the street. It has a pleasant, late afternoon warmth.

4

The following day I decide to reduce Will's gruel ration by half. Carefully I measure out half a cup of oats, which I pour into a bowl. Then I add one and a half cups of water, stir the mixture for a few seconds and put it into the microwave.

As always, some of the oats are floating on the surface of the water, refusing to be part of the mush. In the water I see the reflection of my greying temples. I am fifty and since my retirement (just after the death of my wife from Bright's disease), I have decided that a few mild signs of ageing suit my comfortable domesticity. For the same reason I have lately considered buying a large, quiet cat.

I go to the refrigerator and remove the tin of dog food I opened this morning. Averting my head – I detest the flatulent smell of the concoction – I spoon a medium-sized dollop into Will's gruel.

5

"You expect me to eat that. You really expect me to eat that." Will sounds on the point of tears.

"Top breeders recommend it," I observe civilly.

"You really must be the worst person in the whole world," he says at last.

This interests me. "What makes you say that?"

"You really need me to spell it out?" He is beside himself. "Is this some new part of the torture?"

"No, I'm genuinely interested." I pause. "Still, in a way I can understand your attitude. But look at it like this. I am not really much different from others. Most people care about individuals known to them but merely tut-tut at the mass carnage that they read about in the newspaper. I, however, help the masses and torture only one. More people are helped my way. Compared to those who tut-tut, I am a saint."

And then Will surprises me.

"All right. I'll think about that. I'm sure there's a flaw in your reasoning, and I'm equally sure you'll deny there is one, but I'll think about it." He turns on his side.

6

That night I am woken by a loud crash. I sit up, wondering whether Will has managed to escape. But then I hear the sounds of front doors opening.

I go to the window, draw the white linen curtains.

There has been an accident: a car has hit a power pole. The impact must have been great because the pole is almost at a sixty degree angle, the wires on one side of it stretched taut.

Quickly, I put on my dressing gown.

When I reach the crashed car, I push my way through the crowd of jostling people. I assume that most of them are my neighbours. "Has anyone been injured?"

A man of about my age with an indecisive expression turns to me. "Two people are trapped inside. The twisted metal.... They may even be dead."

"Let me see," I say. "I'm an engineer. I know quite a bit about dealing with metal."

One of the people hands me a torch. I quickly play it over the interior of the car. Inside are a man and a woman in their late fifties. Their faces seem surprisingly dark but then I realise the darkness is blood. I can't, however, see where it is coming from. Pieces of shattered windscreen are everywhere.

I glance back at the crowd. "It won't be difficult to free them. The dashboard is holding them in but if I push it in a certain way, the metal it's resting against will give."

Five minutes later, indeed, the man and the woman are on the pavement, groaning softly. Clearly they will live; and I feel an almost god-like satisfaction at having rescued them.

"You deserve a medal," someone says. "The police still haven't got here. Without you these people could easily be dead."

I nod politely, surreptitiously putting pieces of broken glass into my pocket.

7

It is ten in the morning, and I am in my work room. I meticulously dab my brow and then inspect my handiwork.

I have joined together, side by side, nine boards, so that projecting from their seams are the pieces of glass I collected the previous night. It occurred to me that I have so far been too lenient with Will's sleeping arrangements.

Carefully, I drag the structure towards the cellar. Then I lean it against the wall and unbolt the door.

There is a sudden clank of chains. Clearly, I have startled Will.

"Don't worry, Will." I laugh. "It's no one you don't know."

"Oh God. What is it this time?"

I peer into the cellar. I feel as though I'm looking into a deep well. "I'm not sure you can see it, but it's a bit like... a bed of nails."

There is a sound of choked despair. I wait.

About a minute later, he sighs. "All right. I accept what you're doing. Get it over with. Your argument last night made sense."

Now it is my turn to be startled. "I don't believe it." I peer into the darkness, wondering whether he is planning some silly trick.

"What don't you believe?" His voice is resigned. "As you said, hurting one and helping others is better than helping one and ignoring the rest of the world. At first I didn't see why even one person should be hurt, but then I remembered that that was exactly what God did to Jesus. Who am I to argue with God's example?"

In spite of myself, I am interested. "Go on."

"There's nothing more to say. I accept your argument. Perhaps I've finally lost my mind but what does that matter? Do to me what you will."

For some moments, I stand before him. The cobwebs in the corner are like faint radar dishes. Dust motes spiral like stars.

Slowly, and then with more resolve, I bend to kiss Will's brow. Then I draw over the platform, lift him into my arms and ease his light frame on to the glass nails.

Other Prose @ IP

The Secret Stealer, by *Jess Webster*
ISBN 9781921479397, AU$24.95

A Beginner's Guide to Dying in India, by *JM Donellan*
ISBN 9781921479304, AU$32.95

Willow Farrington Bites Back, by *Rebecca Bloomer*
ISBN 9781921479366, AU$24.95

Wobbles: An Olympic Story, by *Nadine Neumann*
ISBN 9781921479298, AU$32.95

The Hitchers of Oz, by *Tom and Simon Sykes*
ISBN 9781921479199, AU$32.95

Sacrifice, *LR Saul*
ISBN 9781921479168, AU$32.95

The World Cup Baby, by *Euan McCabe*
ISBN 9781921479205, AU$32.95

The Voyage of the Shuckenoor, by *Erica Bell*
ISBN 9781921479045, AU$32.95

Primary Instinct, by *David P Reiter*
ISBN 9781921479021, AU$30

As If!, by *Barry Levy*
ISBN 9781876819804, AU$32

For the latest from IP, please visit us online at
http://ipoz.biz/Store/Store.htm
or contact us by phone/fax on 61 7 3324 9319
or sales@ipoz.biz

LaVergne, TN USA
28 October 2010

202580LV00002B/66/P